Stars IN THEIR Eyes

Pema Donyo

Crimson Romance
New York   London   Toronto   Sydney   New Delhi

CRIMSON
ROMANCE

Crimson Romance
An Imprint of Simon & Schuster, Inc.
1230 Avenue of the Americas
New York, NY 10020

For information about special discounts for bulk purchases, please contact Simon & Schuster Special Sales at 1-866-506-1949 or business@ simonandschuster.com.

The Simon & Schuster Speakers Bureau can bring authors to your live event. For more information or to book an event contact the Simon & Schuster Speakers Bureau at 1-866-248-3049 or visit our website at www. simonspeakers.com.

ISBN: 978-1-5072-0743-7
ISBN: 978-1-5072-0646-1 (ebook)

Praise for Pema Donyo

One Last Letter
"...friendship, broken love, regrets, family, sacrifice, renewed love, and choices ... I recommend this novel to anyone who is looking for a lighthearted, feel-good romance."
—5 stars, History from a Woman's Perspective

"There's romance, and then there's heart-pounding, breathless, fabulous, fantastic romance. Pema Donyo's One Last Letter falls in that category ... I can't wait to read it over again."
—4 stars, The Canon

"...young love becoming true love ... a lighthearted love story with passion. I am looking forward to the next book Pema writes."
—5 stars, Let's Get Romantical

Revolutionary Hearts
"My absolute favorite thing about this book was watching [the heroine] grow. ... You could not use that to hurt her or belittle her if she moved to the point where [her heritage] no longer harmed her. A powerful message for anyone being discriminated or bullied over something they cannot change..."
—4 stars, Once Upon a Dream Books

"It's Donyo's writing that makes Revolutionary Hearts shine ... Donyo's work, from One Last Letter to Revolutionary Hearts, is a must read for any romance/historical fiction lover."
—5 stars, The Canon

Dedication
To the ones who support the ones who dream.

Chapter One

Los Angeles, California

1920

Iris laughed at the driver rolling by in his massive Model T. The middle-aged man shook his fist through his open window as he drove past, exhaust smoke fuming behind his machine. The road expanded ahead of him as clear as day — he had plenty of space to move down Figueroa Street.

A tug on her left hand snagged her attention once again, and she turned her attention back to Owen. He looked toward both sides of the road, then led the way as they crossed the street lined with palm trees. The smell of lye wafted from the entrance of her father's laundromat. She bet if she pressed her nose against her cotton chemise, she could still inhale the scent of fresh soap.

Owen stepped ahead of her, guiding her hand forward. His pressed trousers were cuffed at the ankle, stain-free, beneath his white oxford shirt. She would have been amused at the formality of his outfit under normal circumstances, but they were about to see a film. And it wasn't just any film. It was hers.

A stiff breeze sent a chill up her spine as they headed toward the shade of the ticket box and out of the late afternoon's dull heat. Owen asked for two tickets to *The Red Lantern*. The man at the ticket booth peered at Iris, who stood behind Owen's shoulder. The man frowned. At the beginning of her relationship with Owen, she used to pretend the looks were because she had something on her face or she had worn the wrong hat with her dress. It wasn't because of the shape of her eyes or the shade of her skin. Owen handed her a ticket, and she squeezed his hand.

"For the future star of the screen, Iris Wong."

"Not yet," she said. There was a certain intensity in his gaze that made her cast her eyes downward.

She held her breath during most of the film, waiting for the right moment. Each scene lay between title cards, a black screen with white type explaining what was happening. The pianist below the stage played a soundtrack to accompany the movie, turning his sheet music to the next page every so often.

With each title card passing and each new scene beginning, she edged toward the end of her seat a little more. It was always possible the studio had cut out her scene. And then—there! Her image appeared on the screen, before everyone in the audience to see. The scene was set in an ancient kingdom. Multiple extras crowded the street to await the opening of a palace gate. She stood as one of the lantern bearers, one of only five carriers flanking both sides of the gate. The gate opened and the actor stepped out. Then the camera angle panned to a different location, and she was no longer within the frame. But she had been seen. For the first time, she would be on multiple cinema screens throughout America. A bubbling sense of anticipation filled her chest.

This was the beginning; she was sure of it.

She turned to Owen. When she'd told him about the role, he insisted they see it together. Every time she became discouraged about an audition, he encouraged her to try again. Without him, her dream would have stayed just that: a dream.

"I made it," she whispered.

He nodded and reached for her hand. "Right where you belong."

• • •

After the movie, Owen drove her to his house. They sat on the wooden bench on his front porch. His parents were at a charity function again. He didn't keep many of Iris's belongings at home, but he did have a small pile of her books on his bookshelf for whenever she came over. A person revealed a lot by the way he or she read a book. Whenever he became bored with a story in his latest read, Sherwood Anderson's short story collection, he skipped to the ending after reading the first paragraph. But not Iris. She never skipped around. She read one page after the other, as attentive to each paragraph as the last. Would she be as patient with him?

"What is it?" She rolled to her side, bookmarking her place in the novel with her thumb.

Owen drummed his fingers against Sherwood's leather-bound spine. "Can't a writer admire a muse?"

She poked his side, making him sit straight up on the porch bench. "A muse? I prefer star."

"The star of …" He scratched his chin. "What is your next project again?"

"I've been offered the role of a servant in a short film. It's a start. Douglas Fairbanks is in it." She set the book down, the words forgotten in favor of moving pictures. "Twenty-two might be my lucky year. It's finally happening."

"Have you ever thought about filming outside America?"

"Why would I do that?"

He stood up from the bench and began to pace on his porch. "They say the film industry in Europe might soon give Hollywood competition."

"I can't remember when you suddenly took an interest in film trends, Owen."

He rubbed the back of his neck and stared out at the night. Maybe the view would help him figure out how to bring it up.

Gas lamps lit the winding dirt road leading toward the city. The crooning tunes of instrumental jazz played on the radio behind him, its volume dimmed to prevent upsetting the neighbors. It made the mood feel light, airy almost. He couldn't bring himself to break it.

"Owen?"

She sounded worried. The static from the radio spiked, and then the music stopped. She must have turned it off. Only cricket chirps filled the space between them.

"Remember when I talked about writing a novel?" He leaned against the porch railing to face her, his arms crossed over his chest.

She nodded.

"Well, to do that, you see … All these writers and editors are moving to Paris. And I think maybe if I want to get serious, you know, really write it, I should move too. I want to talk to other writers, hear what they're doing."

Her eyes narrowed. Silence was dangerous when it came to her.

"My father knows a friend in Paris, a writer. My father says I can learn from him. Stay with him for a few months, learn the craft from someone more experienced. Says he has friends involved in the city's literary circle." His shoulders tensed, waiting for the rebuttal.

She clasped her hands in her lap. Her knuckles looked white even under the warm glow of the lamplight beside her. The relentless sound of crickets chirped back at him, teasing him. She needed more convincing.

"Maybe … Maybe you could be an actress in Paris. Then you could come with me."

"What?" She furrowed her brows. "Paris?"

"I'm planning to move there soon. You should join me." He scuffed his shoe on the wooden slats.

"Why?" She raised her voice. "You never mentioned this to me before."

"I was trying to think of the right time to tell you."

He had spoken too soon. This wasn't the proper place to propose it. Not before the end of the year, not before he figured out all the details with his parents. But that didn't stop the hope from swelling in his chest. She could still agree. He waited for her smooth lips to curve upward or her bright brown eyes to twinkle at his idea. He could imagine the two of them bashing around Europe, exploring nightlife in a city he didn't yet understand but wished to know. They could relive the Belle Époque. They could wake up every morning together in the same flat, watching the sun rise over the Eiffel Tower without their parents or society giving them disapproving looks. They could …

"No."

He leaned against the railing with enough pressure to almost topple backward. Anything to keep him upright. "What?"

"I said no." She jutted her chin forward. "I can't go to Paris."

He swallowed hard. "All I'm asking is for you to think about it."

"I don't need to." Her voice brimmed with anger. "How could you ask me to leave my family here?"

"It would only be for a while, maybe a few years. We would come back."

"I don't have 'a few years.' My family needs money, whether that comes from me washing customers' clothes or at the studio."

"It's a part-time gig in the prop department. I'm sure that job exists in Paris. We can send money back home."

"My uncle got me that job, I told you. How am I supposed to find new work?" She crossed her arms over her chest, mimicking his position. Her gaze was glued to the fresh wooden floorboards his father had recently ordered a coat of paint for. "All the films are being shot here."

"Cinema exists in France. There's the theater; there's always something." He was making desperate claims, and she knew it. He closed his mouth midsentence.

When he envisioned life in Paris, he was exchanging narrative techniques and swapping stories with others who shared his passion for words. But Iris had been a part of his life for as long as he could remember. Any life he envisioned for himself involved her in it.

The low hum of a car rumbled behind him. Its flashing lights illuminated Iris's face and caused her to shield her eyes. He cursed under his breath. If his parents had tried, they couldn't have had worse timing. Owen looked over his shoulder at the approaching vehicle. It slowed to a halt before his home. His mother and father wouldn't be happy to find him with Iris so late. He doubted they would be happy to find her even in broad daylight.

His mother stepped out of the car first, a thick mink fur wrapped around her neck. Never mind the temperate weather outside, she always had to make an entrance. Her cool gaze settled on Iris first, then Owen. He sucked in a quick intake of breath. Time to get Iris home.

"Son? Is that chink with you again?" his father's voice called out to him.

He planted his feet on the porch. It was offensive. Iris deserved better treatment. His father's insults stung with fresh force each time. If only he could make his father stop. "I told you, her name is Iris."

"It's fine." Her thin hand rested on his shoulder. Yet when he looked over at her, her expression had darkened.

He gritted his teeth as his parents walked up the porch steps. His mother leveled a look of warning at him. His father, however, tipped his hat toward Iris.

"Good evening, Miss Wong." His tone was calm. "How is your father's laundromat?"

Owen wanted nothing more than to usher her away from his parents and drive far from them. He thought his father would have exhausted possibilities by that point, yet each time he saw her, he thought of a fresh jab.

"My father's business is well, thank you for asking." Her voice never wavered.

His father quirked up an eyebrow. "Still work there, I assume?"

"That's enough." Owen stepped in front of her and met his father's amused gaze. "I'm taking Iris home."

She bowed her head. "I am sorry for staying so late. Please excuse me."

His father gave a curt nod to Owen. "Take her home."

Owen gestured to Iris to walk in front of him. She made her way down the steps and he followed, not daring to look back at his parents. He didn't need to turn around to recognize their disapproving looks. An infatuation with the exotic, his father had called it at first. His father refused to acknowledge the possibility of anything more.

Owen waited until they were halfway down the road and headed back to the city before speaking. "You know I don't care what my parents think, right?"

She stared straight ahead. "You need them."

"I don't," he lied.

"You can pay for your own voyage to Paris?"

He averted his eyes from the road every so often to glance at her. The moonlight lit her pale expression and delicate features. Her nose always seemed to be angled upward, as if above everyone else and rightly so. Yet her thin lips, normally curved into an easy smile, formed a tight line instead. It made his stomach sour. He turned back to the windshield as the car rolled past the adobe buildings that lined the streets. The familiar high domes of the cinemas and parked bicycles along the road lit up with the glow of streetlamps every few yards or so. Shadows covered most of the path and submerged the next street corner.

He slowed the car to a halt. Her house was set deep against the other adobe buildings in a cul-de-sac unreachable by the main road. Even if it had been, he doubted her parents would be pleased to see him.

He let out a harsh laugh. "What excuse is it this time?"

"My friend Paula asked me to go to the cinema with her. We went to her house for dinner afterward and lost track of time."

His name was Paula tonight. Fair enough. He reached for her hand on the black leather seat. She pulled hers away.

"I think it would be better if this is the last excuse I make. At least for a while."

He looked over her shoulder and into the shadows. Did she see her father out there? Was she worried about someone overhearing? But one glance at her told him otherwise. She pressed her lips so tightly together that they almost disappeared into her face.

"If this is about Paris, I promise you: I'll find a way for us both to travel there. Think about it: we wouldn't have to deal with our parents, with people telling us whom we should be with, with any of that. We'd have each other. We'll make it; you'll see."

"You're scaring me. I can't give up my dream just so we can be together." Her voice was firm. "I want to make it here."

He wanted to drive away and drown her out. Then he wouldn't have to hear her. He could keep the memory of their day together unscathed. The impossibility of keeping the memory almost made him laugh again.

"We're going in different directions." The way she spoke was so matter of fact. It was Iris through and through, announcing her decision like one would announce the date. "I've been thinking about it. I still care about you, but if you're going out of the country …"

He swept his hand across the dashboard in front of him, the brown leather covering the huge wheel in the center of a silver scepter. She had called it so the first time he brought the car 'round to her neighborhood. The key jutted out from the ignition, ready to take him home without her. Why had he ever brought up moving? They could have stayed as they were, future unknown.

"Are you trying to say good-bye?"

"I think we should see what happens. Maybe take a break. It's better that way."

"Here? Right now?" He felt numb. Better for whom? Not for him.

"You shouldn't waste your time trying to keep in touch with me when you're there. I think you should focus on the writing." She ran her fingers through her hair, playing with the ends of her bob.

"I'll have time for both."

"Maybe. But we can't control what happens." She hesitated. "You can still write to me, of course."

"I won't be gone long. It's not like I'm asking you to put your life on hold."

"We need to focus on our own dreams. You should go if that's what you want, but I want to stay here." She gave him a sideways glance. Her eyes were wide and solemn. "I still really like you. I do."

Likewise. He couldn't turn off his feelings for her like a light switch. "Then we should stay together. This makes no sense."

"It will." Her tone grew steadier as she spoke. She made it sound as easy as closing a book. "That's the way it has to be."

"I don't agree with this. We could try to make it work." He clenched and unclenched his fists over the wheel. They had something worth fighting for. "Can we at least try?"

"We'll see how it goes." She opened the door and stepped outside. Before she closed it, she paused.

For a moment, he wanted more than anything for her to step back inside the car and forget their entire argument. There would be no talk of the future anymore. They would make plans for the next time they saw each other; they would joke about his father's questions; they would kiss and say good-bye like nothing was wrong.

And then the moment passed. She closed the door with a low click. She closed the door on him, and he drove away from her. As his car rumbled farther from the curb, a heavy ache filled his chest.

Chapter Two

Paris, France

1926

Her first proposal was supposed to come with a brass trumpet playing in the background, white flower petals falling from the sky, and a ring from the man she loved. Instead, she gazed at an empty velvet box and a chap she had known for a few weeks. His eyes looked as round as saucers, imploring her for an answer.

"Cut!" Pierre yelled.

She relaxed her shoulders as her fellow actor stood and closed the box. The spotlights above them shut off. Thank goodness. The heat from the lights was stifling. The cinematographer angled his head away from the camera to tell them they'd done a good job. All routine. She smoothed out the front of her buttercream cashmere blouse as Pierre approached her.

"You make a fine leading lady." He waved toward the film's backdrop.

She followed his gesture to take in the set. It was pure film romance all right, a formerly vanilla gazebo decorated to resemble an oriental shrine. The prop department had strung paper lanterns covered in generic marks that belonged to no language she was aware of. A jade statue of a dragon was placed in the center of the shrine, surrounded by unlit incense sticks placed in open-faced wooden boxes.

It was the Western world's China.

"I'm just glad this role doesn't involve me playing another servant."

She couldn't count the number of Hollywood roles that had been offered to her as the maid. Always secondary parts, never the lead. The last role she'd auditioned for—the role of a Chinese heroine—had been given to an Austrian actress. The role she was offered instead? Her maid.

"Europe needed you sooner. You have wasted too much time in Hollywood." He studied her with the intensity of a sculptor gazing at clay. It sent a thrill up her spine. Hopefully, that look would translate into future starring roles in his films.

She cleared her throat. "Does your invitation to lunch still stand?"

"Of course." He smiled.

Yesterday had been the third time he'd asked her to lunch that week, and the third time she'd accepted. If there was a fourth invitation, her answer would be the same.

The eyes of the film crew and actors rested on her. Let them look. Several of her coworkers had joked about the director's attentions. They teased her about it between takes whenever Pierre was out of earshot. Perhaps there was truth to the teasing. She was in no position to refuse him. If Pierre was interested in her, let it be. All the better for her.

Other actresses waited around for directors or producers to take notice of them. It was the industry standard. It was foolish. Iris had tried the method before to little avail. Why wait? The industry had no room for passiveness. She knew what she wanted. Better that she pursue him. Her next role depended on it.

The production company's studio lay above a street full of cafés in Saint-Germain-des-Prés. Pungent cigarette smoke mingled with the mouthwatering scent of croque-monsieurs. Vibrant petals sprung from the flowerboxes dotting nearly every window of the buildings she passed. Her heels clicked over the cobblestone streets as she caught snatches of French and English around her. The international flavor of the city had surprised her when she'd first arrived a few months ago. Expatriates observed the French and adopted their mannerisms, yet they clung to the safety of their cliques. She had performed in theaters in London and starred in films in Berlin, yet neither city held the same draw for Americans as Paris.

One of her sisters had instructed her to try all the cafés in the city before returning home. An impossible task. She didn't even recognize the current café Pierre drew to a stop before. Its seating area extended outward from the corner of a yellow flatiron building. White lettering spelled out *Les Deux Magiciens* above the enclosure covering half the tables outside. Teal umbrellas shaded guests from the afternoon sun as customers made toasts to the chime of tinkling glass or folded their newspapers with headlines of the stock market's latest rally.

Pierre ordered a bottle of wine once they were seated and then raised a toast to Hollywood's newest star. Her cheeks burned. Hardly, and only if he counted supporting roles as stardom. Still, she joined the toast and sipped from her glass. He polished off his first drink and poured himself another. The hard-drinking spirit of everyone around her was ludicrous. It was drinking for the sake of escape. Whether it was memories of the war or an unpaid rent bill, everyone turned to liquor to withdraw from their problems. There had to be better ways to do so; she was sure of it. It was as if the city transformed everyone into parched sailors, taking in liquor like fresh water.

"There's an excellent collection of cubist paintings at a gallery not far from here." Maybe he would be interested in coming with her.

"Ah."

"It's incredible. An image is broken up and reshaped again. You can guess its original form, but the way it's presented is completely new."

"I see."

"There're dozens of viewpoints with any piece. It shows the object in its natural state, how it should be analyzed, rather than how it's immediately presented."

"That sounds nice."

"Do you prefer any specific forms of art over the other?"

He managed an energetic shrug and gulped his wine.

When she finally gave up trying to gain an opinion from him, he smiled at her and complimented her porcelain skin. She bit the inside of her cheek. His English might not be perfect, but she was sure he could communicate a thought more substantial than one about her appearance.

Still, she returned his smile. Pierre was sweet. And sweet could be enough to sustain a gal for a while, couldn't it? It was enough for her to grin and bear his company for the sake of her career.

"I invited my friend here today, the screenwriter. You wanted to thank him, no?"

She did. Finally, someone had written a part for an Asian actress that didn't portray the heroine as dying for another man or scheming against the hero. The film in Paris would be the capstone to her time shooting in Europe. It would show the studios back home what she was capable of. The rumor mill was circulating news of a potential three-movie contract for her from a major studio; hopefully, there was truth behind it.

Iris clapped her hands together. "I would love to thank him. Where is he?"

She peered over Pierre's shoulder. Perhaps he was already here.

A group of women in cloche hats giggled over coffees at a table. Beside them stood a group of children covered head to toe in wool clothes, selling lilies from woven baskets, waving the fresh flowers toward the women.

A clink of glass hitting marble jerked her attention back to Pierre. He swore in French and grabbed a napkin, dotting his lap. He must have knocked over the wine bottle; the red liquid streamed over the tablecloth and toward him. She righted the bottle as he pushed his chair away from the table.

"Forgive me, *excusez-moi* ... "

"It's fine; accidents happen."

"No, no, clumsy of me, I apologize."

She caught a glimpse of the dark stain on his plum trousers before he headed inside the café, likely to find a sink or at least a pail of water to wash it out.

She traced a finger around the rim of her nearly full wine goblet. The children moved farther down the avenue and passed by her. The mother wielded the largest basket of flowers and used it to gesture across the street. She crossed, and three of the children followed. The youngest, a girl wearing a bright red beret, trailed behind her siblings. Iris winced as the girl tripped against a raised cobblestone and fell forward, scattering her flowers on the ground. Her family ahead of her didn't seem to notice. The girl started to gather the lilies, one by one placing the delicate stems back into her basket.

A canary-yellow roadster sped down the road. Its speed was dangerous on such a crowded street. The girl needed to move. Yet she plucked the flowers from the road without a glance upward. The hairs on the back of Iris's neck stood up. Why didn't anyone help her? The driver made exaggerated gesticulations as he spoke to the woman in the passenger seat, both more absorbed in each other than the road ahead.

Across the street, a tall man angled his head toward the child's direction. He started walking toward the girl, his pace quickening as the car came closer. Iris stepped toward the road, too, yelling at the girl. The child looked up at her. Before Iris could reach her, the man broke into a sprint and pushed the girl out of the roadster's way. The vehicle brushed past them moments afterward, speeding ahead in a tremendous gust of air.

The driver swore and honked his horn. "Get out of the road!" he yelled.

She ran toward them both. The girl was crying, and her remaining lilies lay flattened in the center of the road. Iris crouched down and held her hands.

"Are you all right, dear?"

She nodded, wiping away her tears with the flat ends of her palms.

Quick footsteps followed a cry of Romanian words as her mother joined the party.

She said something to the girl, and the child pressed her face into her mother's thick skirt.

"Thank you," she said to Iris.

Iris shook her head. She wasn't due any thanks.

"Don't thank me, thank …" Her voice trailed off as she pointed toward the man.

Iris supposed she had looked at him before he crossed the street, but she hadn't really seen him. His light brown hair fell over his forehead in soft waves, appearing almost fluffy under the sun's rays. Blue eyes stared back at her in recognition. His shoulders looked broader than she remembered, and light stubble grazed his jaw and upper lip.

"No need to thank me," he said to the woman. He held up his hands as if he wanted no praise. Once the child and her mother started back to the other side of the road, he met Iris's gaze.

He chuckled. "It's been a damn long time."

She nodded, a lump rising in her throat. She had rehearsed so many lines to say to him if they ever saw each other again. An endless cache of words—gone. Images crossed her mind instead:

standing on the dim street as his car pulled away. She had waited until it disappeared around the bend of the road and the rumble of its engine faded away. She would see him again, she'd told herself. Paris was an ocean away; he wouldn't really leave. It couldn't be over. Her legs had burned to run after the car.

"Owen! Is that you?" Pierre waved at them both and gestured to them to join him at the table.

Iris moved as fast as her T-strap heels would take her. Against her better judgment, she placed her palm against one of her cheeks. Burning hot. Hopefully, Owen wouldn't notice. At the table, she ignored the slight shaking of her hands as she poured herself a glass of water.

Pierre clapped a hand on Owen's back. "This is my friend Owen Matthews, our film's screenwriter."

He had changed a bit, at least physically. His arms appeared more muscular. She'd sworn he had been incapable of growing facial hair back in the days when they used to steal kisses on his parents' porch. And the deep tan that had settled over his skin was gone. Or perhaps her recollection of him betrayed her. Her memory blurred the edges, making her unsure of what she remembered.

"We knew each other in LA," Iris said. Might as well be the first one to admit it. Should she have greeted him with a hug or a handshake? Neither? A million questions buzzed through her mind. Maybe he resented her for never writing.

He didn't flinch, just bit into his bread as if she were any other old bird to him. "Nice to see you again."

She'd give up her next audition to keep her cool as well as he did. She gulped down her water, praying it would calm her nerves. Part of her wanted to run back to her hotel and forget she ever requested to meet the screenwriter. She should have looked up his name.

"How did you know each other?" Pierre asked.

"Oh, you know, here and there." She shot Owen a pointed look. The Owen before her was an unknown entity, unpredictable and capable of anything. Besides, it wasn't as if she cared about him anymore. She cared about his perception of her and his professional endeavors, sure. But as a romantic interest? Far from it.

Owen didn't miss a beat. "She wanted to be an actress, even in those days."

She almost breathed a sigh of relief and mouthed *thanks*. The corner of his mouth raised in a half-smile. Damn him, and still as good looking as the last day she'd seen him. Did she compare to how he remembered her? If only he'd run into her while on set, with her glamorous makeup and stylish wardrobe assistants helping her. She looked her best then.

"And she's a brilliant one. I saw her films while visiting America and knew I wanted to cast her myself." Pierre rested his hand on her bare shoulder.

Owen's eyes narrowed at the touch. But she might have well imagined it, because the next moment, Owen smiled at Pierre.

"A real talent you've got there. I'm glad the part's going to her."

The flattery created a knot in her stomach. He had seen her work. She should have kept more detailed notice of his books. "I'm sorry, I haven't heard about your novels. How are they doing?"

He leaned back in his chair, distancing himself from the party. "I write screenplays now."

She widened her eyes. Surely not. It had to be a lie. The Owen Matthews she remembered had loved creating character-driven novels, not churning out action-oriented screenplays. A lot could change in a couple years, but his focus had always been singular. That was what she loved — had once loved, she corrected herself — about him so much. He was the only person with enough determination to match hers.

"Been seeing more activity in screenplays these days," he offered.

His words rang empty. His tone even sounded slightly bitter. She studied Owen's expression, searching for a sign of a joke. What had happened to change his direction?

"And poetry," Pierre said. "He once wrote love poems to my cousin. The smart girl refused him, and the next day he sent the same poems to another girl. This time, she fell for them."

The knot in her stomach grew tighter by the second. She had experienced her share of admirers, and it was only fair he had too. He probably had a wife, maybe even children.

"Is that so?" Iris asked. "Where do you and Mrs. Matthews stay?"

Pierre laughed.

"Right up here, safe in my imagination." Owen tapped his forehead.

Despite his teasing, her chest lifted a little. He wasn't married. She tried to ignore the perverse pleasure she took from the knowledge.

Pierre called over a waiter for the check and then prodded her with his elbow. "Never mind that. Iris wanted to thank you, no?"

Oh, she should have written a note and sent it through Pierre. Meeting the screenwriter in person had seemed like a neat idea when he'd been an anonymous figure. Now, just like when she'd first seen Owen minutes ago, the right phrases left her mind like the cigarette smoke floating above their heads. Words had always been his forte, not hers.

"Right. Yes. I … thank you." She wanted to cover her face in her hands. She could perform in front of a live audience of hundreds of people in London, but she couldn't manage to speak plain English to one man.

He blinked.

"Thank you for your screenplay." She cleared her throat. "It's very difficult to find a role that doesn't stereotype Asians. The way you've written the leading lady presents the character as dynamic for once."

"My pleasure," he said. "I'm sure the part was made for you."

She raised her eyebrows. That was odd. She eyed Pierre to check if he'd caught on, but he was preoccupied with asking for the bill.

Pierre paid the check. She insisted on paying at least half, but he insisted on paying for the full bill. Just like he insisted on walking her to the hotel. She adjusted her weight in her seat, feeling Owen's gaze on her as she accepted both. It didn't hurt to entertain her director. When Pierre tried to link his arm with hers, she hesitated before eventually giving in.

As they stood up to leave, Pierre halted. "Oh! Owen, you must come for a tour of the set. You haven't even visited us at production yet."

He scrawled the address on his napkin and pushed it to Owen's side of the table. Without agreeing, Owen folded it into neat thirds and stuffed it in his shirt pocket.

Running into him hadn't been so bad. Still, if only the wall of formality between them would come down. She was just any other woman to him now. She held her head higher as she walked away from the café. Well, he wasn't speaking to an ordinary woman. She was an actress, a soon-to-be leading lady starring in her big break. All she had to do was work harder than before and stay the course.

A course that did not involve falling for a certain blue-eyed writer again.

• • •

Les Deux Magiciens had been Owen's favorite haunt since only weeks after arriving in Paris, and he still frequented the café to run into friends or meet new writers he admired. The meaning of the place shifted once he saw her standing before it, all clean and crisp in her white dress. He knew her beauty had remained the same; he could see that from all the movie posters outside every cinema and inside every dance hall in the city. Her eyes remained as bright as ever. The only difference was that now the world knew it, too.

No, what had changed was the way she spoke to him. It was all politeness. The easy familiarity of their conversations existed in his memory alone. The reality unearthed a fresh ache in his chest that he thought he'd stitched up. One word from her, and all the stitches ripped out again, leaving him bloody and vulnerable.

Owen tried to press down memories that began rising to the surface. He had no claim to her anymore, hadn't ever had one, really. Her desire to be in the pictures had eclipsed any illusion of their future together. And hadn't he been the one to leave for Paris? He had made his choice with or without her.

He pushed past the thoughts as he stepped into the studio. Pierre's set was on the upper floor of a whole building full of film sets. A crew member wheeled in a collection of fake trees set up on a rolling platform, while another behind him rolled in a massive painted backdrop of a forest. To his right, men in suspenders stood in front of giant panels of light shining onto their set. One man kneeled behind a camera, rolling its crank as he asked the actors to change where they stood. Another man held up a megaphone and commanded everyone to get in their places. To his left, an entire front of a building covered the studio floor to ceiling, complete with a staircase leading to an invisible upper floor and a doorway to nowhere. Extras buzzed about the set as the director gave them all instructions. He recognized the man.

"Pierre!"

Pierre looked around at the sound of his name. When he saw Owen, he smiled and held up a hand. Owen waited by the side of the stage as Pierre spoke to another crew member who followed Pierre as Pierre approached.

"Well, well, looks like you found time to visit our studio after all. I'm honored."

Pierre had an unassuming manner that Owen always liked. There was something genuine about him, trusting even. For example, trusting Owen to write an entire screenplay.

"I was curious about this tour you wanted to show me."

"Ah, I wish our timing could be better. I apologize; I must finish this scene. Alain here will show you around." He gestured to the crew member beside him.

Alain was a stocky boy who looked around sixteen years old. He wore a newsboy cap and a dusty shirt that Owen suspected had once been white. When Pierre said his name, he grunted.

Couldn't Pierre show him around? He held back a sigh. Coming to the studio had been a way to thank Pierre and perhaps ask if he needed any more writing done. And if the writing led to another job that paid enough, Owen wouldn't turn it down. But before he could protest, the cameraman called out to Pierre and the director excused himself.

Owen cleared his throat and said in French, "And what do you do here?"

Alain squinted at him. "What do you do here?"

It seemed they were off to a neat start. "I write. I'm the writer for this film."

He huffed. "And I'm the king of France. Follow me."

Without turning around, he started down the main walkway separating the sets from one another. "To your right is where all the nature scenes happen. Forests, rivers—you name it, we bring it in. On the left are the street scenes. Fighting happens there, the good stuff. Ahead of us, you'll see the indoor sets. I was an extra on the set to our left once. I had a whole thirty seconds. Sometimes we film outside, but it's easier to keep it all in here because you can control the lighting. Plus, it would be a pain to carry all these cameras outside. I'd have to do it.

"And then all that back there—no, not there, to the right of that—is where we keep all the props. I work back there. We're the most important part of the team, you know. Without us, the scene would just be people. Who wants to see that? Anyway, you'll see a ton of rooms along the side of the walls. Those are the dressing rooms."

Owen tried to take in everything at once and failed. The indoor sets looked about the same size as the outdoor ones but with brighter lighting and more props included. The set Alain had apparently blessed with his presence was being used by a team of three men crowding around a camera. One filmed the scene while two others called out directions to an actress. The woman lay on a brocade futon with her eyes closed. Pillows, a flower vase, lamps, a full floor rug, and a screen covered in gold foil also made an appearance around her. The room looked so convincing, he almost forgot he was looking straight into it; the entire other half of the room was missing. That probably allowed for easy access off and on the set.

Each dressing room in the row they passed was marked by a number and a name slipped into a slot on the door.

The boy stood up straighter as a new figure approached them. "Good afternoon, Mademoiselle Wong."

"Good afternoon to you too." Her gaze lifted to meet Owen's. "Nice to see you."

Iris looked incredible. She wore a tight-fitting green dress with a slit up the front of it, revealing her long legs underneath. He tried to keep his gaze upward. "Good to see you too. He was just giving me a tour of the set."

"Is that so?"

"Yes, but I've got to get back to work soon. I was about to drop him off with someone else," Alain said.

Oh, that would impress Iris. It sounded like he was being passed off from nanny to nanny. Who was the adult and who was the child, really?

"How about you get back to work and I'll talk to him?" Iris asked.

Alain shrugged and walked away toward the prop department.

"What do you think?" she asked. She looked at the floor instead of at him.

"It's nice." His knowledge of studios was limited. He'd look like a fool in front of her if he said anything concrete. He gestured to the sets behind her. "It's very … spacious."

She crossed her arms over her chest. "You don't sound impressed."

"Not my world." He gestured to her dress. "You look nice."

"Thank you. I have a scene in a few minutes."

"You play a scullery maid, I assume." He raised his brows. At least they could still joke with each other. He trusted her not to bring up the past, to dredge up those memories again.

She smiled. "Of course. No self-respecting maid would wear anything less than this."

"The new type of maid for the modern era."

"Oh, not that again. Everyone's always talking about the modern woman now, the independent, free-spirited thinker. As if before we were somehow less."

"I'd like to hear more about the modern man. The chauvinistic, backward-thinking modern man. That's what this world needs more of." He was talking nonsense. But judging by the twinkle in her eye, it was a hit.

"And would you say you fit this description?"

"Wholeheartedly. I aspire to nothing less. And would you say that you fit the description of a modern woman?"

"You go tell the press that Iris Wong is the definition of the modern woman. I expect to see it in the papers by tomorrow."

He had forgotten how much self-confidence she exuded. She never doubted herself. The years had passed, and she had grown up to be a woman worthy of admiration, a woman with more determination and success than most. She still burned with a certain fire. He resisted the urge to step closer to her. Better to stay at a safe distance.

Alain emerged from the prop department, his steps quick. He hitched his thumb behind him. "Excuse me, *mademoiselle*, but Pierre is calling for you."

"Thank you. Sorry, Mr. Matthews, I'll have to excuse myself. It was nice seeing you."

He couldn't get out a clever response before she headed in the direction of her set. Alain propped up a foot behind him and rested his weight against the wall. Both watched her walk away.

"She's something, isn't she?"

Alain snorted. "But for you? No chance."

Chapter Three

Cool air blew onto Iris's face. Crew members had propped up giant electric fans throughout the studio, and more and more popped up each day. It wasn't enough to stop her makeup from sweating off her face, despite her makeup artist's valiant effort at touch-ups. She stared straight ahead at a rectangular mirror surrounded in light bulbs and sat back against her elevated chair while the professional worked.

Gabrielle Hallier, a French actress who starred in a supporting role, sat next to her. Her wavy blond hair gave her heart-shaped face an angelic frame. Pierre had told Iris that Gabrielle had auditioned for the leading role, too, but the other actress seemed to hold no ill will toward Iris. She had given Iris recommendations about which streets to avoid walking down at night and which crew members were the best kissers, though Iris tried not to remember the latter.

Gabrielle was, however, not as friendly with the crew members. She huffed as the hairdresser brushed through her hair. "Stop, you're hurting me. Can't someone else do it?"

The hairdresser continued without hesitation. It wasn't the first fit she or Iris had seen Gabrielle throw. When Iris had been in those shoes, all she'd be able to do was put her head down, do her job, and hope no one complained about her. Hairdressers were replaceable; the stars were not.

Once the hairdresser left, Gabrielle leaned in and caught her gaze in the mirror while the makeup artist applied rouge to Iris's cheeks.

"Pierre's looking at you again," she said.

Iris wished she could turn around and verify the claim. "I doubt it."

"Swear on my life."

"Maybe he's looking at you."

"Please. He knows my attentions lie elsewhere." She flipped back her locks over her shoulder like the man in question was watching.

The last she'd told Iris, her attentions lay with the film's sixty-year-old producer. The film's very married sixty-year-old producer. Such behavior had occurred among her friends back home, too. Iris knew better than to ask any questions.

Gabrielle craned her neck to get another glimpse of what was behind them. "Definitely still looking at you."

Iris blushed. Her makeup artist clucked her tongue. The rouge on her cheeks made her look like a clown with the added flush. She couldn't help it. No director had ever paid attention to her before. The ones in Hollywood treated her like an Oriental prop. Pierre recognized her as more. He trusted her with complex facial expressions or dramatic gestures. He believed in her ability to act as much as she did. The reassurance pushed her to perform better.

From behind one of the sets, Alain walked up to their chairs. He worked in her alma mater, the prop department, and as a general messenger boy on set. Her makeup artist stepped back so Iris could greet him.

"Good afternoon, *mademoiselles*."

"Ah, aren't you adorable," Gabrielle said.

He flinched at her description. "Mademoiselle Wong, a package has arrived for you from Los Angeles. It is waiting outside your door."

"Thank you," Iris said. "And don't listen to her. You look very handsome today."

He winked at her. She forced herself to suppress the laugh rising in her throat. No one could flirt with more actresses at once than that boy.

As he had promised, the package lay outside her door. International postage stamps covered the box. Her friends and family had put it together, and her mother had sent her a telegram telling her to expect it any day. The moment she entered her dressing room, she opened the package. Inside was a little piece of home: a small parcel of recent notes from her sisters and parents, a bar of soap her mother had made, a small Buddha statue cast in bronze, a variety of dried snacks she missed, and a notebook. She brushed her hands over the worn leather of the cover. It was her diary from years ago. She couldn't believe that her parents had found it.

The notebook's contents were full of the nonsense she'd cared about when she was a teenager—who was kissing whom, which friends were fighting, who had gossiped about her behind her back. Most of it was embarrassing drivel. But she'd also used it as a folder. Inside the notebook was a collection of different items gathered over the years. A ticket stub to her first baseball game, a photo from when she took her mother to a movie palace, and letters. She flipped through the papers.

One note caught her eye, and she pulled out the wrinkled memo. It had Owen's handwriting. She grazed her fingers over the date: *1919*. He had given it to her on Christmas, and she had read it over and over for weeks afterward. It was from another lifetime. His script was cramped and slanted to the right.

My darling Iris. Thank you for bringing light to my day. I must have done something wonderful to deserve you in my life. I love you very much.

How young and sappy they'd both been. She remembered the passion that had held them together, all-consuming and full of hope. If only she could have those emotions back in their full intensity.

Being around him stirred some of those old feelings again. She recognized it all: the same quickness to his replies, the same tendency to slip into sarcasm, the same unspoken tension that made her stay at least a foot away from him. They had fallen back into a familiar rapport without trying. It wasn't the same; not exactly. Not like before.

Yet her chest tightened as she placed his letter back into her notebook. She couldn't bring herself to throw it away.

• • •

The smell of fresh loaves of bread wafted past Owen's nostrils as he ascended the steel stairwell. He inhaled another whiff of buttery croissants, and his stomach grumbled. Living above a bakery had seemed like a swell idea when he first moved in, yet the location inspired more imagining of the taste of flaky brioche than imagining any characters.

Besides, it wasn't the time to be distracted by his stomach. He had to change into something decent to wear. Pierre had sent him a note inviting him to a cabaret for that night. Judging by his pairing at the café the other day, Owen suspected Iris would be there.

As soon as he entered his apartment, he undid the buttons of his wool shirt and cast it aside on a loveseat. The green velvet had been in desperate need of upholstering even when he'd bought it. Both apartment windows stood reasonably close to the sides of two other buildings that blocked out the sun most afternoons. His oak desk stood against one of the windows to maximize the daylight for his writing. He didn't have the slightest patience for interior decorating, but his apartment had a decent set-up. When he tired of clacking away at his typewriter, he wandered over to the menagerie of stories on his table. Half of the novels scattered across his dining table lay submerged in shadows, their spines sticking straight up to designate their bookmarked spot. The organized chaos matched the variety of artistic styles nailed to his walls. A feast of canvases littered the surfaces, all gifts from friends with a penchant for figures painted in different shades of blue, clocks floating in space, or sharp art deco motifs. Many of them were castoffs from a gallery or unfinished sketches. Just training for a masterpiece.

Owen scanned his wardrobe. A cabaret required a suit. His one suit, to be frank, and one that needed ironing at that. He glanced at his watch. No time. He managed to pull on one sleeve of the wrinkled Oxford shirt before someone rapped on his door.

"Yes?" he asked.

"The rent was due last week, Monsieur Matthews." The landlord raised his voice. "This is the last time I will remind you."

"It'll be here by the end of this week, I swear."

"Remember: I do not run a charity." The footsteps outside his door padded away.

The bill's tardiness hardly warranted anger. Owen prided himself on always coming through on rent payments, albeit one or two weeks late. The check for the screenwriting gig would be in his hands once filming wrapped up; Pierre had promised. The friendly devil had taken his word that he'd written screenplays before and bought this one for a sizable sum. One screenplay sure made a lot more money than selling sketches to magazines, and he needed the funds. His parents had stopped sending him money after a few years. By then, he didn't want their help anymore. He could make it on his own.

Once he donned the wrinkled suit and made a futile effort to smooth it down, he wandered over to his desk. Half-finished drafts of sketches covered the space. His friend Gertrude thought they featured a phantom lady, a woman unseen in the story but lurking in the hero's mind. Owen just used shadows a lot. Perhaps there was a recurring theme in there; Gertrude was often right. After all, Iris served as the model for all the heroines in his work in some regard, whether it was her dark hair or her headstrong manner. No new girl filled the same role as a muse; no other woman came close to inspiring his dialogue. One would almost think it would be mundane for him to see Iris again in person after he spent such significant time with the fictional versions of her each day.

Beneath the drafts lay a stack of envelopes. Bills, mainly. He cringed at the one from his landlord. A reminder to not be late was scrawled in red ink beneath the return address. Well, he couldn't win every battle on time. One envelope stood out among the others: a yellowed one, a bit worn from a journey, and with a "B&L" stamped in elegant typeface along the seal. The logo of the publisher Boni & Liveright.

He tore open the envelope and snatched out its contents. A thin letter stared back at him.

Dear Mr. Matthews,

   While we appreciated the chance to read your manuscript, we regret to inform you …

Another rejection. He crumpled the letter and tossed the scrap of paper into a metal bin next to his desk. If he didn't throw them all away, he could replace the paintings on his walls with rejection letters. Different manuscripts, different publishers, the same answer. The sting no longer left him reeling. He expected it, despite the words of encouragement from friends who found publication or writers who already made money from their advances. Paris placed him among other artists struggling to make a name for themselves. There was something hungry and wild about the city's talent that he found nowhere else. Not in Prague, not in London, not even in the City of Stars.

But he was still taking odd writing jobs, just like in California.

And if he'd stayed in Los Angeles, maybe he and Iris would have never split up. He would be lying if he said he never imagined the alternate future that might have existed for them. Perhaps they would have moved to a house right out of the city, one not too far from her parents and one far enough from his. They would have gone to the cinema every Saturday and read together afterward. When she spoke to him, she would have done so in the same way that had always made him lean closer to her, like an opened gate extending an invitation to all who pass by.

Better to think of an alternate future, a what-if scenario for a world in which she never became unfamiliar to him. He could spend another lifetime dreaming of an alternate future, and it wouldn't land him anywhere. And yet that was the purpose of his writing—to exist within his other world. The one untouched by reality. He glanced at his watch. Visions of a future that never existed could wait, as they always did. It was time to meet Pierre. He looked back at the stack of bills. And time to confirm that his next check was coming through.

• • •

The cabaret Pierre had in mind required creeping through a narrow maze of alleys and street corners between the building and his flat. Once Owen found his way back onto the main road, he recognized the vaulted roofs and shuttered windows marking the street. He had passed through Pigalle before, but he tried not to frequent the neighborhood. It held a seedier cast of characters whom he had no interest to be involved with. Numerous cabarets lined the pavement. Whether in pubs or nightclubs, laughter could be heard from all locations. Piano music echoed into the street. Women wearing dresses that fell barely below their knees leaned against bay windows holding back the gaiety. Each door displayed art deco tiles or hid behind a tapestry of beads. A light breeze blew through the air, sifting the leaves of the beech trees above him.

The city came alive at night.

The closer Owen walked to a man a few paces ahead of him, the more familiar his outline grew. Was that Ezra? His friend stopped before him, his hair as disheveled and voluminous as ever. Ezra walked faster than anyone Owen had ever seen, but a man who did as much writing, editing, and publishing as Ezra would always be in a hurry to go somewhere.

"Wish I could talk more. Wanted to tell you that I liked that last sketch of yours. Gertrude showed me." Ezra straightened his tie. Owen had never seen him stand or sit still. "I'd like to publish it."

Owen wasn't sure which "last sketch" Ezra was referring to, but he had to thank Gertrude the next time he saw her. Ezra had started a literary magazine called *The Transatlantic Review*, and a decent number of talented friends of his had seen their names in publication there. Better than that, it paid.

"How's the novel though? She said you tried B&L."

Owen shoved his hands into his suit pockets.

Ezra frowned. "Better the right rejection than the wrong publisher. If they didn't want your manuscript, someone else might."

He could only wish. He swallowed down his bitterness and shrugged. "Writing's all about rejection. It's a blue business sometimes."

"The color of the business is green. Not depressing blue or sunny yellow." Ezra shook his head. "I think your work will sell. Have patience."

He sounded like Gertrude. She talked of patience like an endless well an artist could always pull from. Owen resisted correcting him and instead thanked him again. At least selling short stories provided another stream of cash.

After Ezra left, Owen continued toward the cabaret. It lay at the end of the street. No one could miss it: a red windmill towered over the building. Crimson and white neon letters spelled out the cabaret's name, casting shadows around the maroon building. Lists proclaiming the night's acts flanked both sides of the entrance. Each window from inside the windmill's building glowed yellow, as if each room were already occupied. Swing music drifted through the exit, where a group of men in black suits stood huddled right outside it. Closer to the entrance, a mural of can-can dancers stood above him. Each dancer held her leg high in the air as her grey skirts billowed behind her.

Owen took off his hat as he entered the building. A flight of stairs separated the entrance from the actual show. The main room was permeated by a swirl of smoke and women's perfume. Red light cast a tint over everyone's face, and even the furniture was a matching shade, making the space pulse with an intense energy. Pinstripe curtains hung above private booths, punctuated by lights that marked the beginning of a larger seating area. Long tables lay before the stage, the closest table crowded already. He scanned the balcony for a familiar face. No luck. He might never find them in the throng.

"Owen! Owen!"

At one of the booths sat Iris and Pierre, heaping plates of black caviar and empty bottles of champagne laid across their table. Relief washed over him. Pierre called his name again, and Owen joined them. Full yards separated the section of booths from the general tables, and groups of men and women continued to stand and talk as the show started. Some even started to dance in the spaces between each plush booth. After all, they had paid for it.

Pierre slurred as he said, "Have some caviar."

"How are you, Owen?" Iris asked.

"Better now that I'm among you two." He lifted a spoonful of caviar into his mouth. And better now that he was among food.

"Did you know, Miss Wong, Owen does not drink?"

"I'm surprised you still don't." She rested her elbows on the table and placed her chin on her folded hands. "Especially among your set."

That firecracker tone of hers was back. "My set?"

"Artists."

"And I'm sure all of Hollywood is dry these days."

"Not drowning in liquor to the same extent people seem to be over here. All anyone does here is drink."

"Maybe you haven't seen the true city."

"Says you! I've been here for weeks. I saw the Eiffel Tower, the Arc de Triomphe …"

"Visit all the tourist spots—what a fine idea. You might as well have seen Paris from a postcard. You know what you need? You need someone to show you around the real spots."

But she had a point. He had seen the effects of drinking among "his set" of artists. It made them act out, forget about their spouses, even forget who they were. Worse, too much drinking or partying could make someone enjoy nightlife a little too much and forget their real work. At the end of the night, they were all in the city for the art.

Pierre raised his glass, swaying as he did so. "A toast!"

Iris caught Owen's gaze and rolled her eyes at Pierre. Owen laughed.

A woman tapped Iris on the shoulder, over the corner of the booth. "Pardon me, miss. Are you Iris Wong?"

Iris angled her shoulders toward the woman and smiled. It was her slow, beautiful smile he recognized from the press. The smile reserved for paparazzi shots and movie posters, not for the likes of him.

"You are, aren't you? My husband will never believe this." The woman pulled out a handkerchief from her purse. "Could you sign this for me?"

"Of course." Iris reached into her own purse and pulled out a fountain pen covered in gold leaf. An actress always came to an event prepared. She signed the handkerchief and handed it back to the woman.

"Thank you." The woman held her handkerchief with care.

It was the kind of moment Iris had told him about once when they were young. She'd wanted to be recognized for her acting, admired even. He'd never doubted her; she had spoken about her dreams with such concrete finality. No one else had spoken about their future the same way. A swelling sense of pride filled his chest. He wanted her to look over at him, but her attention was captured by the show.

The dancer on the stage twisted her feet to the rhythm before a set resembling a tropical rainforest. Her movements started slowly at first and then built up tempo as she kicked her feet in the air forward and backward. She wore a girdle of bananas as her skirt, and a flesh-colored bodysuit covered her torso. A pet cheetah wearing a diamond collar sat to the right of her, watching his mistress move.

Every time she kicked her feet into the air, Pierre hollered and took another sip from his glass. The man drank like a fish. Owen waited until halfway through the dance to lay a hand on Pierre's arm in warning. Pierre nodded yet finished his glass all the same. Not too long afterward, he folded his hands onto the table and lay down his head. His eyes closed within seconds.

"I wish I could dance like that," Iris said.

Owen shrugged off his suit jacket. The heat in the cabaret was stifling. "I would have thought the studios had trained you by now."

"You make us sound like monkeys." She arched an eyebrow.

He smiled. "You said it, not me."

"A monkey without the ability to dance, I'm afraid. Whenever directors see my dancing, they tend to cast someone else."

She couldn't be that bad. He stood up from the booth and held out his hand. "C'mon, I'll teach you."

She glanced over at Pierre. He seemed to be square in Dreamland, his body lifting up and down to the tune of his breathing. A slight snore escaped his lips.

"It seems my trainer has set me free. Why not?" She took his hand through lace gloves.

The touch sent a rush up his arm. He liked the familiarity of her hand's weight in his. They walked over the red carpet and toward the left side of the booth. There was enough space to move about as they pleased.

Owen rolled up his sleeves. "First things first with the Charleston: rhythm."

"Which I lack, I'm afraid."

"Nah, you've got it." He managed a half-smile. How would she react to his mentioning the past? "Though we never danced together, so you might be right."

Iris jutted her chin upward. There she was again, with that perfect, challenging look of hers. "Teach me then, o wise one."

"One, two, three …" He spoke according to the beat of his steps, trying to ignore the big band music swinging in the background. He stepped his right foot forward, then brought it behind him. His left foot followed suit in the opposite order, stepping backward first and then forward again. "Five, six, seven …"

She copied his movements without difficulty. "What's next?"

Eager as always. "Just keep repeating after me … One two three, touch. Five six seven, touch." He repeated the same movement but pointed his toe outward and touched the ground with the end of his shoe both times. Iris followed, holding up her dress as she peered at her own heels.

"Then you twist." He twisted both his feet toward the center then twisted them back out away from him. "Place the weight on your toes, lifting the back of your heels."

Iris repeated his steps, then twisted one foot out, bringing it up from the ground and into the air. "This is the next part, right?"

And the student surpassed the teacher. Her movements did look awkward, but she repeated his all the same at a snail pace.

"It's usually done a little faster than that." He moved alongside her, quicker than the speed she displayed. "Here, let's try it to the music."

He danced in front of her, trying to set a rhythm. She started to dance faster as the trumpet's blare picked up the tempo, her steps moving to the beat. She couldn't keep up with him at first, but eventually her movements began to mirror his. Their steps moved in sync. Her slim figure seemed to glide over the floor as she danced, and his body drew closer to her. She didn't pull away. The next time the Charleston refrain repeated, the snare drum echoing through the cabaret, Iris threw back her head and laughed. It was a sound he hadn't heard in years.

As the song wound to a close and transitioned to another, one with a slower step, Owen stopped dancing. They stood before each other, panting. He grinned. A certain magic surrounded her, an aura of independence. She didn't seek out people; they sought out her. He had the feeling that she floated wherever she pleased, untethered to everyone and enchanting whoever happened to be in her way.

And he was the lucky bastard tonight.

Behind her was a small balcony. Several balcony enclosures dotted the back of the booths, allowing higher-paying guests a view into the courtyard below.

He pointed to one. "Want to get some air?"

Her long skirt fell back to the floor in a small train as she followed him. He had always admired the way she carried herself. Even in school, she'd walked with her shoulders thrown back and her posture straight.

The balcony's view looked out onto the well-trimmed gardens. The cabaret's owners had built a maze of flowers and shrubbery below, around the outskirts of the maze, and he was sure some backdoor exit would lead them down there. Electric fairy lights and soft candlelight flanked both sides of the walkway. The wind pressed cool against their cheeks, and the thin sheen of sweat dotting his face faded away. Outside the chaos of the cabaret, the dips and rises of the brass instruments' song from inside grew dim. He faced her, leaning against the railing as she stared at him from the other side of the balcony.

"Do you miss LA?" he asked.

"I miss my family." She cocked her head. "Do you miss it?"

"I miss the people. My family visits me here, so I can't say that."

"Which people?"

You.

"Friends," he said.

One element he hadn't missed was her ability to look right through him. She still looked at him that way, skepticism staring back at him. "Tell me really: how's the writing been?"

He cracked his knuckles.

"You can be honest with me."

"Not everyone's dream happens as easily as yours."

"Easy?" She scoffed. "You think it's been easy? Baloney! Remember when I thought being an extra in that lantern movie was the most exciting thing in the world? I was such a sap. I knew nothing about the industry. You have no idea how hard it is to gain even supporting roles." She sighed. "I take what I can get. These days it's either an exotic Polynesian dancer or a Native American princess in distress with two lines of speaking parts."

Her ability to land contracts with major studios was impressive, regardless of the role. Then again, this was Iris. She never settled for less than the best.

"I know I can do more," she continued. "It's a matter of the right part and the right film. I have to wait."

"The most beautiful actress in Hollywood stuck in another supporting role. A damn shame."

Her cheeks flushed. "I'm hardly the most beautiful."

"Did I say the most beautiful? I meant the most funny-looking."

She laughed at his response. He would do anything to hear it again.

"Stop teasing. Hopefully Hollywood takes notice." She waved a hand in dismissal. "Enough about me. You haven't told me about how your writing is going."

The girl never gave up. "Rejections, mainly."

Her eyes softened. He couldn't stand another look of pity. He preferred judgment. He wanted her to be angry about his failure, furious even. Not pity him.

"But not all bad. Published in a few magazines." He tried to keep his tone light. "Still trying to get a book into the world. Rejections till then."

They both stared out at the gardens as the sound of the jazz behind them grew louder. A soprano voice lilted through the windows.

Iris's voice was low. "I always thought you would reach your dream before me."

His shoulders tensed. He wasn't sure what had inspired her sudden mention of the past. Besides, she was the more determined one between the two of them.

"The way you spoke about writing was unlike anyone else," she continued. "You would get inspiration for a story, and then you were off writing for who knows how long. It was like nothing gave you more joy."

He used to feel the same about her love for the movies. It felt good to hear someone talk about the old days. To be honest, he might have been more productive while living in LA than before coming to Paris.

"The city's full of distractions. When I used to work with my father's friend, he kept inviting me to all these events. People always tell you to come with them somewhere, meet someone they say you have to meet …"

"And you feel like if you don't attend, you're missing out on another opportunity to make a connection that could make your career."

"Exactly. And then you do go, and it ends up being another event where—"

"You're talking to people full of themselves who talk in abstracts about your work. And all you can do is ask yourself is how this is supposed to help you."

He studied her, half expecting to see sarcasm. But her face held no trace of mockery. She meant what she said. Finally, someone who understood. They had spent time on different sides of the world and yet lived parallel lives.

She faced the garden. "You supported me a lot when we were younger."

If this was her idea of an olive branch for calling off their relationship, it didn't quite reach across the years.

"I always regretted not supporting you more. I was so angry when you moved." Her hands tightened over the silver railing. "But I get it now. We both did what was best for us."

He rubbed his jaw. What could he say? Nothing seemed right. This conversation could lead down a long road. It was overdue. Every word she said whetted his appetite for more.

Clang!

The sound came from behind them. He whipped his head around to see a waiter scolding Pierre, both his silver tray and bowls of caviar strewn across the floor. The director waved his arms as he shouted.

Iris pulled away from the balcony, a lost look on her face.

Owen suppressed a groan. Perfect timing. "I think our friend over there needs to head home."

Pierre continued trying to speak over the ragtime tune blaring from the stage. Owen apologized to the disgruntled waiter and guided Pierre to sit back in the booth. Soon enough, he settled into a sluggish state. He rested his head back over his arms as if to sleep. *Not so fast.* Owen tried to rouse him by prodding him in the shoulder. No response. He shook him until Pierre scowled and shoved him away. *Better.*

"Do you know where he lives?" Owen asked her.

"I do. I'll take him back."

Ridiculous. Pierre's weight would crush her. He leaned toward Pierre and shrugged one of his arms around the director's shoulder and grabbed Pierre's waist to steady both of them. Heavier than he expected. Iris stepped out of the way for them, and he angled his head in the direction of the exit. She led them down the stairs, looking back over her shoulder every once in a while to make sure they still followed her. As they left the cabaret and rounded the corner, he started to slow his steps on purpose. He would drop Pierre off, she would head toward her hotel, and then what? He didn't want to let her get away again.

Chapter Four

Iris closed the door to Pierre's flat. She knew the location from a cast party he threw before filming began. For a while, she had feared that she was leading Owen astray as they wound through the narrow streets. Pierre looked like a hefty load to support. Nevertheless, she heard no complaints from Owen until they arrived at Pierre's door. At first, Pierre refused to take out his keys. His sober behavior reminded her of a sweet bore; his drunk one reminded her of a difficult child. After goading from both Iris and Owen, he finally agreed and allowed them to set him down onto his sofa. If her past conversations with him were anything to go by, he would wake up in the morning with a terrible headache and few memories of the night before.

She and Owen stood outside the flat. "It seems this is good night," she said.

"It seems so."

She clasped her hands behind her back. His posture was equally rigid, his shoulders squared. The magic of the night had faded. In the cabaret, she could have almost sworn no time had passed between them. While they were dancing, a sense of weightlessness filled her. All the expectations and barriers she saw for herself faded away. Now "good-bye" was an easier word to think than to say.

"Thanks for your help bringing him back."

"Of course." He leaned against the trellis propped against the wall. Ivy wound through its crisscross pattern. "Does this happen every night or only when he wants to impress you?"

"No, thank goodness." Pierre's behavior had been appalling. When she met him at the cabaret, his breath already stank of liquor.

Owen gave a low whistle. "Nice place he's got here. You stay in a flat like this?"

"My hotel is a block away. It's decent."

"A block away, hmm?" He ran a hand through his hair. "Would have offered to walk you home, but a block isn't too bad."

Darn, why hadn't she let him walk her without telling him the distance? Here was her chance to say something else. Talking with him felt so familiar; surely the night didn't have to end. She bit her bottom lip as another thought crossed her mind. At the same time, he had no reason to stay with her. He had plans to meet up with another woman, for all she knew.

"Good night then, Iris."

Say something. Stop him from leaving.

"Good night, Owen."

At least they parted as friends. She walked away first, her heels clipping against the cobblestone street. Maybe he hadn't left yet. She looked over her shoulder. Her heart sank. He had walked away, headed in the opposite direction. She faced the road ahead of her. A fortuitous run-in, that was all it would be.

"Iris?"

She stopped. To her left, a shop window showed her profile in its reflection. The window also showed Owen walking toward her, his pace slowing as he approached. She turned around. Maybe she had forgotten something.

"Do you have plans for the rest of the evening?"

Or maybe not.

"Because I was thinking that if you're not busy, there's a gathering of some of my friends in Montparnasse." He studied her expression. "If you're not busy."

When Iris had started accepting interviews with reporters, she'd learned an important trick: if it mattered, never say yes right away.

Saying yes right away could lead to the interview being canceled at the last second. Saying yes right away could lead to the interview being an hour long but only two lines of a quote in the paper. No, it was better to draw it out. And that meant not actually saying yes right away and jumping up and down in elation, which was what she wanted to do.

She met his gaze and faked a confidence she didn't feel. "Your 'set'?"

He smirked. "You could say that."

"Well, I was planning to rehearse my lines for the next shoot."

His head hung a little. "You're right. It's fine."

"But I suppose I'm already dressed to go out. And it doesn't take long for me to rehearse."

He wiped his palms on the front of his wrinkled trousers. Did his hands feel as sweaty as hers? Being around him made her senses heighten. She strolled beside Owen along the dim avenue as her nerves continued to build. She wanted to spend time with him, and he wanted to spend time with her. That was it. No reason to second-guess her decision. She was tired of planning every move she made ten steps in advance.

A full moon lit up the night sky and exuded a rim of white shadows around it. The ominous clouds covered a portion of the moon. The apartments they walked past obscured the lamplight, casting shadows onto the street. Her face slipped into and out of the shadowy light while he remained on the brighter broad avenue.

"You look like a woman of mystery," he said.

"Hardly." Yet she made no move to walk closer to him. Better to stay at a safer distance.

The generous shadows provided her with protection. At least this way, he couldn't see the idiotic smile stretching across her face. She snuck a look at his hand, hanging loose by his side. It felt odd to walk next to him and not take his hand or feel his fingers intertwine with hers. She missed the simplicity of it. Other lovers took her to bed after a couple drinks or let their hands roam too far south while dancing, their touch always feeling like an invasion. Blame it on youth or nostalgia, but with Owen, it had always felt right.

She tried to remember the last time they'd held hands. If she had known it would be the last time, she would have held on tighter.

• • •

Owen regretted inviting Iris as soon as they entered Gertrude's apartment. It wasn't the décor that embarrassed him. Her antique fireplace crackled with a warmth that matched the host. On the mantel stood the completed works of every respected English author and a Russian one as well, sandwiched between two wooden bookends shaped as bulldogs. A Persian rug woven from swirling patterns of gold thread lay before the fireplace, with plush cushions propped up toward the end of it. Someone had swept the heavy amber curtains aside for the night to reveal the streets below. The open window carried in the buzz of pedestrians even at the midnight hour. Twinkling in the distance stood the familiar outline of the Eiffel Tower, appearing more like a miniature toy than a towering guardian of the city.

What made him question his decision was not the room itself but its contents. Everyone was long gone into their liquor; he should have known better than to arrive so late in the night. He swore that a living room used to be next to the doorway, but it had been converted with a platform. Canvases mounted to easels formed a half-moon on the stage. Guests approached the platform and painted on the canvases, sometimes painting over the work done before. Macaroons had been placed at equal intervals along the edges of the platform. One painter stepped on a macaroon, shrugged, then picked up the crushed concoction and ate it.

A group of his friends formed a half-circle around Scott, who was doing an impression of what Owen assumed was an elephant. He blared a bestial cry and stormed around the room. When he and Owen made eye contact, he let out another bellow and headed Owen's direction.

"It's been forever since you joined the fray, boss. I'm acting out Gertie's latest poem. Care to join?" Scott's gaze shifted from Owen to Iris. "And who is your companion tonight?"

"Ignore him." Gertrude elbowed her way forward to stand in front of Scott. "My poem references an elephant, and he has taken liberties with the material."

She placed her hands on her hips and looked Iris up and down. Owen had told Gertrude about her before, and he wasn't sure how to explain himself. But the woman had tact, unlike most of their friends. She exchanged introductions and pulled Iris and him aside, insisting on introducing them to everyone. There was the trumpet player from a jazz club down the street, the groundbreaking surrealist currently working as a telegraph operator, the heiress and art patron who deserved more than her flat tire of a husband (Gertrude was sure of it). Each person she introduced them to sounded louder than the one before. Someone turned on the radio, shifting past static to find bits of music floating in and out of the frequency. Another guest had written the lyrics to one song, so it had to be turned up to full blast. A welcome distraction. He took advantage of it and broke away from Gertrude.

Iris followed him to the back of the room. They walked past several guests in various stages of undress playing poker around the dining room table.

"Your friends are lively."

They were worse than Pierre. "If you want to go home, I understand."

They stopped at a small wooden table behind the poker players. She sat down across from him and shrugged. "Trust me, I've seen worse back home."

Relief washed over him. She would stay, at least for the moment. "This is them when they're boring."

She laughed. "Do you remember when you picked me up from the studio once and I said my day had been boring? And right then a man walked past us covered in pink beads?"

He did remember. Both the man's pants and his shirt had been covered in beaded fabric. All the lights on set had reflected off the clown.

Owen might not have recalled what he had said, but he did recall the rest of that day. They had been dating for a little less than a year back then. He'd picked her up early from work so they could drive to her favorite ice cream shop before it closed. It was the middle of January, and she had been insisting on the treat for days. He kept telling her it was a ridiculous idea, but he bought ice cream for them anyway. Her smile when she finally held the cone in her hands made up for the coldness of his. He itched to bring it up. Yet it waded into forbidden territory, part of the boundary he could not cross. Did she remember the rest of the day as well, or could she somehow revisit her memories without including their relationship?

She laughed again.

Hopefully, the years between them hadn't suddenly given her an ability to read minds.

"What's so funny?"

"I can still remember you saying, 'Never a boring day in Hollywood.' I think of that whenever I see someone dressed in beads." She traced lazy fingertips along the edge of her collar as she spoke.

He followed its path south, toward her dress's plunging neckline. It exposed the swell of her breasts, their outlines disappearing into the low-hanging fabric. She had gathered up her skirts as she sat down and propped out one leg to her side. The tanned skin begged his gaze to trail upward to the shapeliness of her thighs, covered halfway by satin cloth. He missed the way their bodies once molded together, the comforting weight of her hips pressed against his. She would curl up next to him, warm and soft and familiar. If he edged forward, he could kiss her.

"I believe one of your boring friends is trying to get your attention," she said.

A clap on his back jolted Owen's attention upward, where Ezra stood over him. The entirety of Paris wanted to prevent him from talking to her alone that night.

Ezra gestured to the empty chair beside them. "Mind if I sit down?"

"We were actually talking …"

Before Owen could finish, Scott wheeled in beside her. He adjusted his tie and whispered something into her ear, then addressed Owen himself. "And I wouldn't mind a dance with this lovely actress of yours, boss. It's not fair you get all the good ones."

She gave Owen a sidelong glance. "Is that so? How many others am I competing against?" Her voice sounded amused.

A slow song filled Gertrude's apartment. He assured Iris over the noise that there were none, but it didn't stop Scott from extending his hand out to her. She shot him a questioning look yet accepted Scott's hand. She had the right to do what she wanted, yet why with him? Jealousy flared in Owen's gut as she laid her head against Scott's shoulder while they danced. Scott didn't deserve her. Then again, no one in the room did. He sure as hell didn't.

Ezra's face obstructed his view. His words tumbled out fast and energetic. "I apologize for my curt behavior earlier. I was in a rush. I wanted to talk to you about your story."

He tried to look behind Ezra's head at the dance floor, but Ezra matched his movements. He gave up. "I'm listening."

"There was something about it that gripped me from the beginning."

Owen raised his eyebrows. Part of him had suspected Ezra might be publishing him as a favor to Gertrude. After all, his work paled in comparison to the others publishing in Ezra's review.

"It's the sharpness of your language. It sheds all sentiment of the Romantic period. There was a scene after the one outside the bar— what was it again?" He snapped his fingers, as if the move would reignite his memory.

"Inside the hero's apartment."

"Right!" Ezra pointed at him. "Your words were direct."

"I'm trying for a clearer style. Precision works best. Do you think I should have included more description of his internal thoughts, though? That might have needed work."

"None of that needs to bog down the narrative. Cut, cut, cut, that's what I believe." He made slashing movements in the air as he spoke.

A frenetic energy built within Owen, the kind that only occurred when he was talking about his craft. He found fuel among the city's community. Everyone wanted to immerse themselves in their art. Everyone wanted to learn from one another and feed off the other's energy. The city had opened his eyes to a world of inspiration. It came at a cost, though. His friends poured most of their energy into dancing and drinking, not creation. The city worked as an oasis for writers to pass through, but it was a difficult place to get actual work done.

"Paris needs your voice."

"Hardly. It's crowded with enough writers," Owen said. "Do you ever think about leaving the city?"

"And go where? London?"

"Back home."

He frowned. "And do what?"

"Write, still." Owen pedaled backward. It seemed the bustling pace of life in Paris still matched Ezra's tastes. No use pushing the subject. Ezra might think he wasn't serious about staying in Paris and change his mind about publishing Owen's sketch. "Never mind. I'm glad you like the story; I could use the money. Landlord's been bothering me about rent again."

"Rent! I could use a payment if anyone's offering." A man Owen recognized as a friend of Ezra's joined their table, plopping into Iris's former seat. "Or a patron."

Another man leaned away from the poker table to join the conversation. "Oh, be quiet! You have an inheritance to fall back on."

"All these writers with endless flows of inheritance money are the ones who irk me," Ezra's friend said. "They type three words a day and spend the rest of it in leisure. Writers like us are the ones who have to work at it."

"And the price of everything keeps increasing," the poker player complained. "It's all these people trying to get into the city."

"You could always take another job." Ezra's tone had cooled. "You cannot write if you cannot eat."

And that was exactly how the screenwriting job had come about. He hadn't told Ezra about it, but he wouldn't be surprised if his friend already knew. Pierre had offered him a life raft to keep him from drowning in his expenses. And he owed Pierre nothing in return except a story.

He didn't like the way the director had looked at Iris at the café. His throat tightened. Perhaps he did owe Pierre something else as well. If Pierre was interested in Iris, Owen could step out of the way. Besides, the director could provide her a life much better than he could. An exuberant townhouse, starring roles in films, reservations at the finest restaurants. All Owen could offer her was a collection of rejection letters from the finest publishers. Damn, what had he done by inviting her? It had been a foolish decision.

Iris walked over to Owen. "Now it's your turn to dance," she said.

"I'm fine."

She tugged his sleeve toward the floor. But he remained in his chair. He wasn't in the mood to dance. She knelt in front of him as the others around his table left to seek fresh entertainment.

"I'm sure we could show them the Charleston and impress them all." Her warm breath tickled his cheek. "We could put on a show."

"I don't enjoy being made a spectacle."

She clasped one of his hands in hers and tried to pull him toward the radio. Despite his desire to follow her, he kept his hand limp. No use dancing with someone who belonged with someone else. It would give him hope for something that would never happen. When she finally dropped it, he shoved his hands into his pockets. Her eyes searched his, trying to look through him again.

"Scott told me that he thinks you're a talented writer."

He brushed it off. "It's the alcohol talking."

"I doubt it."

"You can't judge it if you've never read it."

She pursed her lips. "Well then, I would love to read some of your work."

He had shown her bits and snatches of his writing when they were younger but never a complete story. Would she recognize herself in his stories? More importantly, would she find her recurrence flattering? Unsettling, more likely.

"You should; it's excellent." Ezra popped his head between the two of them.

Owen waved him away. "I'll think about it."

Ezra let out a huff and turned toward the mantel. When he returned, he unfolded a parcel of papers from a manila folder. Gertrude had once told him that the man never went anywhere without a copy of the latest stories for his review, but he hadn't imagined it to be literally true. To his chagrin, Ezra pulled out a stack of twenty or so pages of typewritten work and handed the pile to Iris.

"I have my own copy at home." He shoved the parcel back under his arm. "You should let more people read your work, Owen. A writer has no use for modesty."

Owen watched him retreat to the rest of the party. The man had a proper education and not one lesson in minding his own business.

"Now you've done it," Owen snapped. If she read his story, she would recognize herself as the heroine. What if it scared her away?

She frowned. "What have I done?"

"Forget about it."

"Tell me."

"I said, forget about it."

"All I want to do is read your work."

"That's not necessary."

"It is if I want to support you."

"It's a bit too late for that, don't you think?"

She stiffened.

His tone had come out sharper than he'd intended. "Forgive me."

She ignored him. "I need to be up early tomorrow. I think I'll head to my hotel."

She rose from her chair, clutching his story at her side. There was a pinched expression on her face as she averted her gaze from his.

He stood up at the same time. "Let me walk you home."

"Thank you, but I can manage on my own."

"Allow me, please."

"Good night." She brushed past him and walked toward the door.

Maybe he wasn't good at the whole "being friends" scenario. When it came to women, he preferred to end interactions with a clean break. Spending time with Iris came with loose ends. They'd had their chance once before, and he'd ruined it. She had no reason to reciprocate his feelings, not with prospects like Pierre. He thought of the papers she had held in her clenched fist, wrinkling the front page. Even if his behavior didn't terminate it, their renewed acquaintance would end with a fell swoop once she read his story.

Owen watched her walk away for the second last time.

Chapter Five

Iris had read a script once about a man who wanted to travel the world in a ship. His wife sold everything she owned to allow him to afford it. Once he bought the ship, he sailed off without her. The director had found it all terribly funny and offered Iris the role of the wife's servant, with the important task of selling all the wife's items.

No wonder her father had disapproved of how she'd spent her time.

When she first returned to her hotel, she wasn't sure what to do with Owen's story. Half of her considered throwing it into a drawer and forgetting about it, especially after how cold he'd acted toward her. It was like a complete change had come over him while she'd been dancing with Scott. One moment she'd sworn Owen was flirting with her, and the next moment he couldn't wait to be rid of her. It was as embarrassing as being invited to a callback audition only to be rejected for good. She had deluded herself into thinking he might still care.

But his story burned a hole in her drawer and her mind. Seconds ticked by on the clock. Curiosity kept her tossing beneath her sheets even while she closed her eyes. After nearly an hour of inventing endless possibilities of what it could be about, she went to her hotel's living room and opened the drawer. She would read just the first page, enough to satisfy her curiosity. That would be enough to send her to sleep. Yet the first page's sentence continued onto the second page, and the second page's paragraph continued onto the third. Before long, she found herself on the last.

Slivers of sunlight dappled across her floor. No use trying to sleep anymore. She made herself a hot cup of coffee and settled against her mohair sofa, the pages of his work scattered before her on the low table. She gathered them and fanned the pages out as she sipped from her cup. Scott was right; Owen was an excellent writer. His style was clear and concise. His language held no trace of the flowery Romantic poets she used to read. In his story, every word belonged.

She warmed her hands around the mug as she watched the sun rise over Paris. Its rich amber hues coated grey buildings and softened their hard edges. Wispy white curtains framed her window and blew into the room, giving a dreamy effect to her suite. A group of pigeons cooed as they settled onto the windowsill, reminding her of the early hour. She should be rehearsing lines, not reading a story.

The premise was simple. A man and woman meet. He falls in love. The woman possesses a lifelong dream to touch the stars. The man buys her a ladder, and the woman climbs the ladder, only to realize that it's not high enough to reach the sky. Next, the man builds her a tower. The woman makes it to the top of the tower and, to her dismay, she still cannot reach the stars. Then he buys her a hot air balloon. Navigation proves impossible by night, and he guides the balloon back to the ground. Finally, the man admits defeat and tells the woman he can't help. She sees a shooting star head toward them and catches it. She never needed him in the first place.

Iris's eyes settled over a passage: the vivid description of the heroine. She had black hair that unfolded to her back, bright brown eyes, and a slim profile. She rambled at times. She worked at her father's business.

Iris scratched at a prickly feeling underneath her skin. Hope could be dangerous. Yet the feeling expanded in her chest without warning.

Owen had written about her. Owen had written about them.

She set her cup on the glass table. The noise almost startled her, awakening her from a fog. She gathered the papers and placed them in a neat pile on the edge of her table. Enough analysis for one morning. She was late for work. If his heroine could touch the stars, so could she.

• • •

Beef carpaccio, pig pluma in raw salt, roasted filet of hake with spelt risotto, "patte bleue" chicken of 100 days. Iris read down the brasserie's menu with a sinking feeling in her stomach. Somehow, she doubted she could order bacon and eggs.

"A very modern menu, no?" Pierre said.

She nodded without enthusiasm. It might have been, for all she knew. She needed a guidebook to translate it.

Fruit stands and pastry shops lined the Rue du Faubourg-Saint-Denis. The chic restaurant stood in front of a paved courtyard right off the avenue, beneath a shielding porch that looked like it was about to cave in any day. The staff bustled about tables covered in spotless white cloth. If not for his reservation, she doubted they would have found a table. A massive mosaic glass dome loomed over the heads of the guests, making her feel small. Pastel murals of pastoral scenes covered the walls. Pierre sat across from her, his back pressed against the leather booth. Above his head was a painting of sheep flocking together amid otherwise barren grassland.

She yawned. Even staring at it was enough to make her feel tired, and her lack of sleep the night before didn't help.

"You seem quiet. Are you all right?" Pierre laid down his menu.

"Fine." She straightened her shoulders. "Tired, that's all."

"Well, when filming wraps up at the end of the week, you will have a welcome break. I have plans to travel to Los Angeles as well."

"I would be happy to show you around."

"Then let me return the favor. I have booked a hotel suite downtown. It's quite large." His voice lowered. "You would be more than welcome to share it with me during my stay."

Maybe she was imagining it, but she doubted living with him as a platonic friend was what he had in mind. She feigned a smile. "I have my own apartment. And my family lives nearby."

He placed his hand over hers. His touch felt clammy. "Maybe a weekend visit, then. Let me know soon."

It made her right temple throb whenever someone told her to "let them know." She would decide on her own time, especially when it came to men. She knew both actors and actresses who slept with casting directors or producers. Some landed major film roles with the said directors or producers afterward. Whether it was by asking or due to affection, she didn't know. She slid her hand out from underneath his and used it to call over the waiter. This had been what she wanted, hadn't it? She finally had Pierre's affections. Yet the idea of sleeping with him made her stomach churn.

The waiter arrived, wearing a long white shirt over black pants. A black vest and black bow tie completed the look, making him look more penguin than man. He pulled out his notepad. "And what can I serve for the lovely couple tonight?"

"*Confit de canard*," Pierre said.

"Do you have grilled chicken?"

The waiter narrowed his eyes at her. She would take that as a no.

"I'll have his order as well then," she corrected.

The waiter snapped his notebook shut and took their menus. "Wonderful. Are we celebrating anything tonight? An anniversary, perhaps?"

The only event she would be celebrating was leaving the restaurant. They were not a couple, and there would be no anniversary. She placed her hand over the side of her face, shielding her pained expression from the waiter. Pierre told him they were not but thanked him all the same. After the waiter left, Pierre returned to staring at her cleavage, like the waiter had been an interruption rather than a welcome distraction.

"A lovely couple, no?"

No, she wanted to reply. Still, a small part of her wished she could agree. She found Pierre attractive; that wasn't the problem. His hair still looked boyish, strands falling over his forehead at odd angles. Light stubble grazed his jawline. If he had any acting ability, he could star in his own movies as the hero. But talking to him was like talking to a beautiful wall.

"Our new film is progressing on schedule. Almost wrapped up," he said.

She stifled a yawn. "Indeed."

"How did you enjoy the city?"

"It's lively. I think I'm ready to return home for now. You're the local, how do you see it after all these years?"

"It's all right."

She drummed her fingernails against the table. "How so?"

"Same old city to me. As long as you like it."

"You're a flirt tonight."

"I am all seriousness." The corner of his mouth twisted into a smile. "I am serious about you."

She scanned the restaurant around her, averting her gaze from his. Clusters of lights shaped like flowers hung from the ceiling and shone onto the checkered tile floor. They sat in the first room of the brasserie—known as "Paradise," Pierre had told her—as opposed to the back room, where less famous guests were seated. From the Paradise room, one could see every customer who came in through the front door. She watched the entrance, scanning the guests for a familiar face. Perhaps one from Gertrude's apartment.

His voice sounded dry. "Is there someone else?"

Owen's face flashed through her mind. "Of course not."

He looked unconvinced but didn't press the topic further. Their meals soon arrived. She tried to make progress into her dish. But the duck didn't smell as fragrant to her as Pierre seemed to think it did, and the vegetables tasted bland. It was his turn to keep up the conversation that night. He talked of his next holiday to Switzerland he had planned, and she paid attention at enough intervals to murmur in agreement.

She sat inside the nicest restaurant she had ever seen and yet had no desire to be there. Was Owen at a similar place with another woman? Was he writing his next story? His pages still formed a small pile at the end of her table. She heard his low voice behind the words, whether reading the man's dialogue or describing the heroine. She bit her bottom lip. Other men gave her plenty of compliments, and yet none of them provided the warmth that Owen's did. And even then, compliments were the least important thing she cared to hear from him. She wanted to know what inspired him to write, how he remembered his home, what was on his mind.

He still intrigued her.

Pierre cut into his roasted duck and took another bite. When he spoke, small bits of roasted meat shot into the air. "I've been chosen by the same studio to direct another film. They're looking for a lead actress."

"Where?"

"Here, in Paris."

Her parents sent her frequent telegrams, asking her when she would be home. She missed them. Her half-year tour of Europe closed out with Pierre's film, and she had promised her family that she would be back. Part of her wondered what would happen if she stayed. It was easier to be an Asian actress in Paris. The same prejudices didn't exist; the phrase "yellow peril" never crossed movie posters. Most of all, it was thrilling to have starring roles for six months. But at the end of the day, the film industry still revolved around Hollywood.

"Thank you for telling me. Right now, I'm hoping for a leading role in LA."

He swallowed down a large bite. "I know directors in Hollywood. Maybe not the major directors you work with, but they would be open to meeting you with my recommendation."

"In what roles?"

"They've worked with Hayakawa and Aoki and given them top billing. I doubt they would turn you away."

Her heart lifted. Sessue Hayakawa and Tsuru Aoki were Japanese actors, married, and two of the few Asians in Hollywood alongside Iris. She'd seen Tsuru in films growing up, watching her in the leading roles Iris herself craved. If certain directors helped them, maybe they would help her too.

Pierre pointed his fork at her, a half-chewed vegetable at the end. "One's even making talkies."

Talking pictures were all anyone in the industry discussed anymore: sound films with dialogue instead of cue cards. A full-length talkie? Hard to believe. Nevertheless, Iris was thankful that her time in Britain had involved speech lessons. She had shaken off her Californian accent in favor of an English lilt. If talkies caught on, maybe that would make her more attractive to directors.

"That would be wonderful."

"Excellent. I'll do what I can for you."

She shifted her weight in her seat. Goodness, she couldn't refuse him when he held her next career move in his hands. He might not recommend her to his connections in LA. Besides, there was always the possibility of work drying up and her returning to Europe. Refusing him might mean burning a needed bridge. It wasn't worth it to reject his advances, not yet anyway. She would maintain the friendship they had. Even if that required tolerating looks that were a little friendlier than she desired.

Pierre laid his hand over hers again. Alarm bells rang in her head as he stroked his thumb over her skin.

Her eyes widened. Tolerating touches was a different matter. She moved her hand out from under his again, this time tucking a lock of hair behind her ear as an excuse. Why not take it one step further? She held the side of her head, feigning a headache.

"You should rest," he said.

"You might be right. I'm not feeling very well."

"I'll walk you home."

"No, no, I'll be fine." She opened her purse and pulled out the required number of francs to split the bill. "Thanks for your suggestion. I'll head to my hotel."

He pushed the francs toward her end of the table. "Nonsense. Let me pay."

Perhaps she was racking up an invisible debt in his mind. What if he thought everything came at a cost? All the times he escorted her home, all the meals he insisted on paying for, even the roles he brought up. She stood from the table without taking the money.

But she had no intention of heading to her hotel. She needed air. A cool breeze blew through her hair as she walked out of the restaurant and toward the Seine.

There was no real night in Paris. Not night in the traditional sense, the one in LA where everyone went to bed (at least she did) at a reasonable hour and the clubs closed before sunrise. In Paris, everything stayed open later. The streets could be more crowded at 3:00 a.m. than 3:00 p.m.

She strolled along the bank, her shawl wrapped tight around her shoulders. A row of benches lined the river. Elderly couples huddled together while artists sketched the serene view onto square notepads. She squinted at the drawings, trying to determine what they were. Some sketches could have been photographs, others looked horrendous. For example, the man sitting on a bench ahead of her drew fast, yet his picture was hopeless. It looked like either disfigured train tracks or a gnarled vine.

She stopped walking. Hold on; she knew him. The man was Owen.

• • •

Owen discovered around the age of twelve that writing was one of the few hobbies that didn't involve people. Playing baseball involved confrontations with the umpire. Trading baseball cards was almost as bad; someone doubted the value of your card or you had to haggle. He was too young for the bars and too young to drive, so he wrote instead. The characters in his stories never expected him to go to law school, like his father. His heroes never fought with him for a girl, like his supposed friends. His heroines never left him for someone else, like his first girlfriend. When he was in his imagined world, he could forget about the real one.

The same could be said for drawing. He was no talent at sketching by any means. But whenever the words jammed in his brain or all the sentences he punched into the typewriter stank worse than the city's sewage, he picked up a sketchpad. Armed with charcoal and a square notebook, he marched down a flight of stairs and toward the main road. Two turns left and half a mile later, a view of the river greeted him.

Wrought iron benches stood at regular intervals before a fence. If he left home on time, he could catch the sunset and attempt to capture the movement along the water in black and white. Sometimes he tried to draw the scene before him without the small fence that surrounded the perimeter of his view. The new expats would stop behind him and ooh and aah, amazed at seeing a real artist at work. The locals would sniff and pass him by without a second look: There were better views of the river; this was an amateur.

Streetlamps created rays of light that flickered across the water. Some nights, he drew the flashes of light themselves. Some nights it was the trees flanking both sides of the bank. Sometimes it was the nearby lamppost, which obstructed a decent portion of the view to his left. Never the people, though. He had enough of those to deal with.

He tried to focus on the detail of the fence, etching its outline onto paper, as if that was what occupied his mind. Had she read the story yet? Iris was busy with her filming; the chances were slim. If she had read it, the chances were even slimmer that she'd liked it. He slashed across the page, forming the crisscross pattern in the center of the fence. Yet maybe she had. Maybe she was impressed by what he wrote.

A clip of heels edged toward him. "Owen?"

He looked up and his gaze locked with Iris's. She wore a white shawl around an otherwise dark evening gown. The attire looked more fitting for a ball than a walk. Her hair brushed against her cheeks, flying at odd angles due to the wind. Her cheeks flushed pink from the chill. She was beautiful.

"Hello," he said.

"Hello."

"I … I wanted to apologize for how I acted the other day. I wasn't myself."

"It's fine." She closed the distance between them until she stood by his side. "I read your story."

"Oh, that old thing." He rubbed the back of his neck. "What did you think?"

She glanced farther down the avenue ahead of them, then back to him. She bit her lip. "Would you … would you want to walk with me?"

"Right now? Well, sure."

"Good. Let's walk. I'll tell you."

He folded his sketchpad and placed it under his arm. If a walk was what it took to hear a review, so be it. He stuffed the charcoals back into his pockets. They strolled alongside the Seine, listening to the gentle splash of the waves lapping against the walls.

"It needs more work," he said. "It's a bit too simple. I could use another round of edits."

"It's wonderful."

He couldn't stop the slow smile spreading across his face. "Really?"

"I loved the way you described each character's determination. They felt like real people."

He could listen to her compliment his work all day. "I'm glad you liked it."

"There was one thing, though."

"What?"

"The end. It was a little sad, don't you think?"

He kicked a stone ahead of him, sending the pebble skidding across the cobblestones. It bounced twice, then it stopped. "Not every story has a happy ending."

"But you're the writer. This is your story."

"And it shapes itself. Fine. What would your ending be?"

"One where they both get what they want."

"Not very realistic."

She wrinkled her nose. "The woman holds a shooting star at the end. How realistic is that?"

He laughed.

"Fine. Leave the poor man unhappy."

"That wasn't what I intended. The characters do what they want."

"I think every person wants to be happy."

"No one knows what's going to make them happy, though."

They rounded a bend in the road, leading away from the main avenue and into a narrow street. The river followed them, the wide expanse continuing into what seemed like an endless trail. When they turned the next corner, the river could no longer be seen. An intricate iron gate marked the end of the narrow alley. With both sides flung open, it guarded an arch that led the corridor toward a shopping district. The moonlight cast a bluish coat over the limestone buildings. On one side, signs hung from windowsills that marked galleries, bookstores, and music shops. The other side of the street held tailors, grocers, and attorney offices. It was like the two faced each other down every morning, trying to prove who was more necessary.

"Enough about my make-believe," he said. "How's the filming going?"

"Done at the end of the week."

His chest constricted. So, she would leave soon.

"I'll miss it, this city." She waved toward the closed shops. "But I'm ready to go back."

Los Angeles. He could still remember those palm trees swaying slightly in the afternoon sun, still feel the dry heat that surrounded the city. It'd felt like a prison when he left. Right now, it felt like home.

"Do you ever think about returning?"

"Sometimes," he said.

"Would you?"

She was full of questions tonight. It would be nice to see his house again. Maybe work for a newspaper while he tried to write. He suppressed a sigh. Christ, he was kidding himself. If he returned to Los Angeles, he wanted to be with her.

He gazed through the shop windows, hoping she would change the topic. A few storefronts remained lit despite the hour, mainly from boutique galleries the owners lived above. These midnight galleries relied on the drunken purchases of tourists who stumbled through their doors. Most held cheap art, replicas, knockoffs that unwitting visitors believed were a bargain. Even if the stores were open, the majority looked abandoned. The hour was too early for the drunkards.

A dead end marked the road ahead of them. One had to walk through a building that led to the other side of the street. The building consisted of a small corridor with a vaulted ceiling. Two chandeliers illuminated the otherwise dim passageway lined on both sides with rusted benches and tables topped with chairs. Imposing portraits of nobles glared at anyone who walked past. The other side partitioned stores by paint job: the first store, a bakery, was painted a stark white, and the second store, a gallery, was painted a flaming red.

He peered inside the gallery. Iris stepped ahead of him, examining the room. The first floor was a massive studio. The gallery owner sat in a corner of the room behind a desk. The old man's head rested over his folded arms on the desk, his whole body slumped in a leather armchair. He didn't stir as they walked past him and toward the rows of paintings. The gallery displayed much of its art behind gilded frames. Low-hanging chandeliers illuminated the images, and shadows flickered against the walls. Yet several paintings stood propped up on wooden easels in the center of the room. Flattened objects stretched out in deformed proportions covered most of the canvases. Stools stood before several of them, like the artists had stepped away for only a moment.

"I think we're the only ones here," she said.

He followed her to the end of the gallery. Toward the back, rows of bookshelves held framed miniature portraits inside them. The back wall held an alcove, a rounded half-dome set inside the cherry wood walls. Against the wall, the owner had propped up a sofa covered in faded velvet. She slowed as she approached it.

She looked at her clasped hands. "Was the woman in the story based on me?" Her voice was low.

There it was. He ran a hand over his jaw. She was right, of course. Yet he still had some pride to hold on to. "Not sure what gave you that idea."

"Not me right now. Who I used to be. The version of me that you remember."

"I wouldn't say you've changed too much."

"I could say the same for you." Her smile was bitter. "Not much has changed at all, has it?"

The scent of floral perfume filled his nostrils as she stepped closer. It was becoming harder to concentrate. *Friends, they were only friends.* He'd had his shot; she deserved someone better. But damn, how he wanted to kiss her.

He tried to change the subject. "When do you leave?"

"Next week."

So soon. If he faked bravery, maybe he would feel it. "That's good. You'll get more filming done. It's better for your career."

"My career." She sighed. "There's quite a long way to go for me."

He missed the starry-eyed gaze that used to shine in her eyes whenever she talked about show business. She had all these grand plans for the types of films she would star in. He could imagine her on his front porch once more, waving her hands with flourish as she acted out a scene in a recent movie. The Iris who stood before him might laugh at the girl he remembered. Yet she had completed more movies than he could recall. Every time he saw her on another poster or screen, a sense of pride filled him.

"There's not much else I can do. Last year I auditioned for a role for an Asian lead, and it went to an Austrian actress."

"That doesn't make any sense."

"But it's the business."

He couldn't stand to see her look so upset. "When you go home, at least you'll see your family again."

"And you'll be here."

His heart raced. "I'll still be here if you return."

Paris may not have provided all the opportunities it had promised, but it was where all his contacts lived. Outside of Paris, no one knew him in the publishing world. She would leave, and he would stay. He had been given a taste of time with Iris, and it would leave him all the worse for it once she went back to America. She had existed as a series of fond memories before, almost his own creation. But given the last few days, she had become as real as anyone around him. The idea of saying good-bye made his stomach tighten.

For the briefest moment, he allowed himself the pleasure of imagining what would happen if she stayed. There was enough room in his flat for both of them. They could attend Gertrude's parties and make fun of his friends. He would introduce Iris to his favorite spots in the city. The vision grew hazier after that. His imagination deflated. She wouldn't be satisfied in Paris, not when so much of her life was in California. Not every story could have a happy ending.

"I don't know if I will," she said. "Six months away was too long. My family misses me."

"Of course." He forced a hardened edge to his voice. "You should be back home."

"Then we might never see each other again."

"We will." The words rolled off his tongue before he could consider them. He didn't know if he believed them, but they might reassure her.

She took a deep breath. "I still think about that night."

He froze. She had to be talking about the night he mentioned Paris. He could stop her before she brought it up. It would save him from reliving any more heartache.

"It wasn't perfect, you know," she said. "I didn't like the looks people gave us or the way your father talked to me. Then you brought up Paris, and I was scared. If I held on to you, I would be holding on to a fantasy. I didn't want to commit to something so far away. I thought you wouldn't come back."

In the weeks afterward, all the time he used to spend with her suddenly became vacant. She had said they would stay friends and yet never reached out to him. That was when he had missed her the most. And what had he done to distract himself? Bought a ticket on a steamer headed straight for Europe. It was an impulsive decision. By the time the weight of missing her hit him in full force, he found his feet planted on French soil. Even when he wanted to make it up to her, he was an ocean away.

"We were both to blame," he said.

"Don't say that." She paused. "I used to think about life in Paris, sometimes."

Her words stung. It was almost easier to imagine that she grew tired of him or wanted more independence and drifted away. Nothing was worse than imagining what could have been and knowing that she envisioned it too. Which of them regretted that night more?

"Do you ever think … if I had joined you, we might still be together?"

He hesitated. "We might have."

"So I ruined it."

"No, no. You didn't ruin anything."

"Then why do I feel like I did?"

"You didn't. It was a long time ago."

"What would you do if you were in my position?"

"I would go back home."

"But what do you want?" She looked up with wide eyes. "Would you like me to stay?"

She reached forward and interlocked her fingers with his. Their palms pressed together. The shock of her smooth skin on his felt foreign, almost surreal. He searched her expression for an explanation. It had been a long time since they'd last held hands. They fit well together; they always had.

He wanted to leap with joy. There was a chance for him even among the Pierres of the world. The warmth of her touch spread through his arms and filled his chest. He brought her toward him and wrapped his arms tightly around her. Could she hear how fast his heart was beating? How he'd missed this. Her soft skin pressed against his made his heart race. He inhaled the flowery scent of her hair as he buried his nose into it.

He could ask her to stay. Yet regardless of how he felt, he couldn't forgive himself if she made a decision because of him. If he asked her to remain in Paris, he'd be holding her back. Hollywood deserved to know her. The world deserved to know her.

She pulled away. "It's too late."

"We still have time." It was limited, but she hadn't left yet. He would take what he could get.

"Days. That's hardly anything."

"It's enough."

It dawned on him that the night might be one of the last times he ever saw her, independent of a screen or poster. He tried to memorize her image. She looked so fine standing before him in the alcove, staring at him beneath her full lashes.

His kiss was soft at first, then more insistent. His hands settled over her hips, pulling her close as he deepened the kiss. She leaned into it and his shoulders relaxed. The gallery faded away as their focus narrowed on each other. He would deal with the future later. In that moment, he wanted to stay with her for as long as he could.

He drew away. "Would you like to go somewhere else?"

"Yes," she said.

They walked out of the gallery, her steps quicker to match his pace. After a while, the streets and buildings looked unfamiliar. Sweat gathered at the base of her palms. They were headed back to his apartment; they had to be. A knot formed in her stomach, but she kept her strides in time with his. She wanted this. She wanted him.

When he closed the door behind them and kissed her once more, she gave in. They'd wasted enough time already. Her body molded against his as they stumbled toward his bedroom between frantic kisses. She unbuttoned his shirt in seconds while he peeled off the straps of her gown.

Chapter Six

Iris stretched her arms out over the sheets. The haze of sleep covered her brain in a fog as her eyelids flickered open. Sunlight streamed through a small window above her, casting diagonal rays of light on the blankets.

She opened her eyes fully as the sleepiness subsided. The brightness betrayed the late hour. Yet the room had poor lighting, which fell on a certain space of his bed and left the rest of the room dim. Paintings covered most of the walls, though some hung at odd angles and a few looked like simple sketches someone might have doodled on a napkin. No other furniture stood in the bedroom, aside from an oak wardrobe with a simple door. The bed she slept on was smaller than the one in her hotel. The box springs on the mattress poked into her back. Then again, a comfortable sleep hadn't been her primary concern.

It was tempting to stay here, to quit struggling. All dreams of being a leading actress seemed far away as she lay in the bed. Her goals were ten-foot walls to scale barehanded, while the alternative was sleeping in. Yet how many others gave up their dreams in laziness?

Iris's stomach rumbled, interrupting the reverie. She had a lunch meeting with Pierre to discuss the final scene. She could pretend to still be ill. But that wouldn't do. Filming was scheduled for the next day, and she couldn't miss it. Another lunch with him was fine.

Furious tapping rapped against a typewriter. The noise drifted from the living room. She walked to the doorway and leaned against it. To the far side of the parlor, a desk stood against a window. It blocked a significant portion of light from entering the room and yet focused brilliant sunshine onto the desk's surface. Owen sat hunched over behind it.

She loved watching him work. Each key made a punching sound as he pressed it, striking the ribbon to place words on the page. When he neared the finish of a line, a small bell chimed and he pushed the return lever into position for the new row of text. His fingers worked with a steady rhythm. He never paused to take a break but never allowed his hands to fly over the keys either.

She placed a hand on his shoulder. He finished the sentence before taking her hand and kissing the top of it. It was as if they had stepped back in time for a morning. How long would it last?

"Good morning," he said.

"Mmm, yes, it is," she replied. "What are you writing?"

He turned to look at the paper, as if surprised it was there. "Not sure yet. Just an introduction for now. I wanted to bang something out."

"If you ever need a reader, I'm willing."

"I'll keep that in mind."

He stood up from his hard-backed chair and kissed her forehead. The sweetness of it caught her off guard. She wrinkled her nose. He wrinkled his own in response, and she laughed. She pecked a kiss on his cheek, and he made a contented sound from the back of his throat. Somewhere, in the back of her mind, she recognized it.

"How did you sleep?"

"Terribly. Someone kept waking me up. I don't know who it was."

"I don't remember you complaining."

"I'm not. Being woken up was quite enjoyable, I'd say."

His smile reached his eyes. It made her feel light.

"And what would you like to do today?"

"I'm supposed to meet Pierre for lunch." As soon as the words left her mouth, she wanted to take them back.

His shoulders stiffened.

"We have a meeting. He wants to talk about business." The words didn't even sound innocent to her. Oh, why had she brought it up? She could have left without telling him where she was going.

"All right."

"It's only lunch." The room felt cold. She wished for her shawl again.

A lump formed in her throat. She wanted to stay in Owen's flat and allow him to kiss her as much he wanted. She wanted to sit on his sofa and catch up on all the years they had missed. But she didn't live in a bubble. No one could have everything they wanted. Declining the lunch risked offending Pierre. And offending him risked losing any connections or roles he could offer her.

"When do you have to meet him?"

"Soon."

"Are you leaving now?"

She kept her eyes downcast, focusing on the ridges of his floorboards instead of Owen. She would have to answer if she looked up.

He stepped back. "Last night happened, you know."

"Yes, it did. But I can't just say no to him."

He started pacing in front of her, moving in quick strides up and down his parlor.

"He's offered me so much. It would be ungrateful to decline him."

"I understand."

"Owen, don't be upset."

"I'm not." His tone failed to convince her. "I understand what's happening here. Go ahead, go back to him."

"That's not it."

"You're right. It's not. It's his connections, and opportunities, and …"

She raised her voice. "How dare you."

"He's connected. And rich. What did he promise you, huh?"

"He's your friend. How can you speak of him that way?"

"He's a friend who offered me work. That's as far as our relationship goes. Tell me, what kind of work does he offer you? Which actresses does he mention?"

She crossed her arms over her chest. "I am very grateful for what he's given me, and I would like to continue to preserve our business partnership."

"If that's what it is."

She narrowed her eyes. "What are you talking about?"

"This is about you wanting to be a star and him promising that to you. And I can't give you that. That's what this is."

"Take that back."

"Why, because it's true?"

Her blood boiled the more Owen railed on. He made her sound like some sort of fame-hungry monster, spreading her legs for a role. She hadn't even slept with Pierre, for goodness sake. Goose bumps rose on the back of her arms. And yet she had spent the night with Owen without any thought of professional gain. It scared her to death.

"This conversation is over. I'm leaving."

"Fine."

"You have no idea how hard I've worked to get here. To know people like Pierre. I can't burn down all those bridges because you decide to waltz back into my life."

"I'm sorry," he deadpanned. "I thought last night meant something."

"I thought so too." She walked back to the bedroom to retrieve her purse.

He followed her to his room. "You're better than this. You don't have to live at his beck and call."

She found her purse and tucked it under her arm. Owen stood in the doorway, blocking her way. She tried to push through. He wouldn't budge.

She gritted her teeth. "Just because you haven't achieved your dream doesn't mean I can't still try for mine."

His jaw went slack. The fire in his eyes died out. When she tried to push through him again, she met no resistance. Her footsteps slowed as she entered the parlor. She had said the worst thing she could think of. If only she could take it back. She didn't mean it. He knew that, didn't he? She turned around. He still stood in his doorway, stunned.

"I didn't mean that," she said.

The only noise was the grandfather clock in the corner of his room, filling the valley between them with repetitive ticks. She couldn't leave like this. He would only associate her memory with arguments. So many wonderful memories, and they would end it with anger.

"Are you going to the wrap party?"

He kept his gaze fixed on the floor.

A sinking feeling settled in her stomach. Why couldn't everything between them untangle, until all that was left was the two of them? No complications. Another wish in the collection of many. Without looking back, she opened the door and walked out of his flat.

Chapter Seven

The sheets still smelled like crushed lavender after she left. Owen had to wash them and hang them out to dry before he could get a decent night's sleep again. He blamed that and wondering whether she shared a bed with Pierre.

For the rest of the day, he kept writing—a furious clacking of the keys. She had chosen to leave. Any effort on his part to go after her might scare her away or, worse, just cause her to leave him again. If she wasn't ready to speak to him, he wouldn't push it. And besides, he didn't know where she was staying. He couldn't ask every hotel in Paris whether a guest named "Iris Wong" had taken up residence. Every few hours or so he would glance at the door; had he heard a knock? Maybe she would come back. She had left her cashmere shawl on his sofa during the fight. She had to return to collect it. He would open the door for her as if nothing was wrong and take her into his arms. She knew where to find him.

Another day passed in the same manner. Still writing in his parlor, still glancing at the door. And he waited. A knock at the door came on the third day.

Owen shot up out of his chair and glanced in the mirror. He smoothed his hair back. Presentable enough. As he opened the door, however, the smile faded.

Pierre peered into his apartment. "A cozy place you've got here. Could use a little more light."

"What brings you here?"

He ignored his question. "Invite a pal in, would you?"

Owen stepped aside. He didn't need to tell Pierre to make himself at home. Pierre roamed around his apartment, picking up stray pages to glance over them or leaning close to the pictures on the wall.

"Say, you seem to be in a sour mood. Writing not going well?"

Terribly. He cracked his knuckles to prevent snapping at Pierre. "How have you been?"

"Good, good. Filming, mainly." A slow smile spread across his face, and Owen wanted to wipe it off. "I have been seeing Iris a lot lately."

He loosened his collar. "You and her, huh?"

"I hope so. She is exquisite, don't you think? A true talent."

"She's something, all right."

"Tell me, what was she like when she was younger?"

"Well ..." He took a deep breath. "Just as determined. Just as confident. Sometimes, it seemed like all she had to do was put her mind to something to make it come true. She was fearless. She was ... unstoppable."

Pierre gave him an odd look.

Owen wanted the subject to change, and fast. "And what do I owe this visit to?"

"Ah! Yes, didn't want to do this outside." He reached into his jacket and pulled out an envelope. "This, my friend, is your payment for the screenplay. Good work, couldn't have done it without you."

Finally, a paycheck. The unpaid bills stuffed in his desk called out to him.

"But before I give this to you, I must make a request." Pierre waved the envelope in his hand. "Are you attending the wrap party tomorrow?"

He'd never heard of one before Iris's invitation. No doubt it was yet another one of Pierre's lavish parties. She would be there, no doubt. And likely not wanting to see him. If she wanted to reach out to him, she would have done so already.

"It might not be a good idea."

"You've turned into such a hermit lately. It'll be good for you. You can't stay in this cave all day."

His tone was insistent. Owen's gaze settled on the envelope. One night seemed like a low price for another payday.

"Fine."

"Wonderful!" Pierre handed Owen the envelope with a triumphant look. "Here you go. Make sure to dress up a bit."

Little relief washed over him as he accepted the check. Dressing up was the least of his worries.

Pierre wandered farther into the parlor, as if looking for something. He stopped by the battered sofa. Owen followed his gaze. Across the seat of the sofa was Iris's white cashmere shawl.

"I've seen this before." Pierre picked up the cloth for a moment and inspected it. "Doesn't Iris own a shawl like this?"

Owen's mind raced. "She might."

"Why do you have it?"

Telling the truth wasn't an option. He doubted she wanted Pierre to know about that night. *Quick, think of an excuse.*

"Oh, it's not hers."

Pierre dropped the shawl back on the sofa. He looked relieved. "Oh?"

"It's … mine." He faked a smile. So much for quick thinking.

"You wear shawls?"

"It's a trend I'm trying out, yes. They go with most of my clothes. Want to try one?"

"I'm fine." He raised his eyebrows. "You always were a little odd."

Better odd than caught. Owen waited for Pierre to leave before he stuffed the shawl into the bottom drawer of his desk. He suppressed a groan. He would never hear the end of it. There went being considered a serious writer.

• • •

When Iris was six, her parents had given in and allowed her to buy a movie ticket. This was back when they used to live on Flower Street, a block north of Chinatown, in a neighborhood that her mother used to refer as a "big stew": Chinese and Germans and Irish and Japanese, all immigrants with a nascent claim to the land. More important to Iris, movies surrounded the neighborhood. On her way to school, she would see cameras cranking and films being recorded. A Nickelodeon theater stood midway between her home and her father's laundromat.

As a child, she would pass by it while walking with her mother to the laundromat. She would tug her mother's hand, begging to go in. At first, her mother disagreed. It was a waste of money, she said. But Iris's determination was relentless. Bright, illustrated posters and ornamental lights covered the windows to attract visitors. To her, it looked like the entrance to another world. And when her father finally gave her a nickel for helping at the laundromat, she knew how she wanted to use it.

Her mother accompanied her to the theater. The bare walls and hard wooden seats may have distracted her, but all Iris needed was a black screen and a piano to the side. When the music started and the first cue card appeared, she was transfixed. The pictures moved before her eyes, weaving a story for her alone. It was about a telegraph operator who saved the day by capturing bandits who tried to rob the telegraph office. The whole film couldn't have lasted longer than fifteen minutes, and she felt the injustice of it as soon as the screen went dark. Once her father gave her another nickel, she went back to the theater for another screening.

She even missed school one time to see a movie. Her teacher made her stand up in class and tell everyone where she'd been. She said she was sick. When the teacher asked if anyone else could vouch for her story, Owen was the only one who stood up. He was one of the few who accepted her. He didn't give her wary looks or tell her that his parents told him not to talk to her, unlike the other kids. From that day onward, she invited him to watch films with her. It was her escape. An escape from the girls who teased her for bringing rice to lunch, an escape from the sweltering heat trapped in the laundromat, an escape from the windowless bedroom she shared with her sisters.

At least she could afford the escapades now. She pushed her round frame sunglasses farther up the bridge of her nose as she paid for her ticket. Last time she went to a theater without them, someone recognized her in the line. Recognition was nice but not the reason she chose to go alone. At least once a week, she sought solace in the dark comfort of the theater. No one knew who she was, and no one expected anything of her. All she had to do was enjoy the film's magic.

The cinema she selected for this afternoon was situated along the Rue Victor Cousin, only a block or two from the Sorbonne. The neon lights above the entrance, though unimpressive by day, formed the shape of a red camera by night. The cinema's interior held no resemblance to the grand movie palaces she frequented at home. Its main room looked like any lounge in a modern household. Plush sofas stood next to dusty lampshades reflecting the light emitted through the mosaic glass windows. She followed the crowd of people down a narrow hallway and into the theater.

Maroon seats covered in velvet upholstery formed seven lines in front of the screen. Yellow seats were scattered throughout the maroon, either as a splash of color or as a furnishing mistake. Plastic curtains lined the walls, as if they would part ways and reveal separate screens behind them. The screen before her couldn't have been much larger than the one she remembered from her old Nickelodeon theater. She sat in the row second to the front, the best one as far as she was concerned. Not so close to the screen that she couldn't see anything but close enough to immerse herself in the film.

For a moment, she thought she recognized a man walking down her row. She removed her sunglasses to get a better look. Sweat gathered at the ends of her palms. Dark hair, muscular build, broad shoulders. It had to be him. But as he came closer, her hope dimmed. Not Owen after all.

Wonderful—she was imagining him. She avoided the man's quizzical look and reclined in her seat. What was she to do about Owen? There was always the option of doing nothing. The thought felt almost reassuring to her as the movie started, the projector whirring somewhere behind her. It always left a little something to be desired when no piano was playing to accompany the film. Yet what the movie lacked in sound, it made up for in color. The brilliant yellows of the stage steps contrasted against the deep green leaves of the film's backdrop. There was a kind of magnetic pull that existed between her and the screen. She could still remember the first time she told Owen that she was determined to work in the industry. She wanted to bring its magic to viewers and provide others with an escape. What could be a more noble profession than creating magic? He had agreed.

The movie focused on a young choir girl rising to stardom as a performer in a nightclub, but the real reason Iris (and everyone else in the theater, she suspected) had come to see it was because of the famous cabaret dancer who had a supporting role. The dancer shimmied her way across the stage, waving her arms in exaggerated movements.

Iris often tried to pick something from the actors to learn from, but there wasn't much to glean from this role except for dancing. More dramatic films allowed her the opportunity to learn a new facial expression or notice the way the actors interacted. She used to try to reenact her favorite scenes with Owen sometimes, putting into practice whatever she'd gained from her critical study of the film. He would even tell her when she did something incorrectly. He'd watch her practice again and again until her delivery matched the way the actress had delivered a line.

After those informal rehearsals, the sun would set and the night breeze would start to cool the desert. If they were lucky, his parents wouldn't arrive till later in the night and they would have the kitchen to themselves. He would make two lemonades, and she would spike hers with his father's vodka. They would talk for another half hour until the drinks were downed. Then she'd lean across the table and kiss his sticky lips, tasting the remnants of his empty glass.

The lights lifted in the theater. She looked around. The screen was dark. Children nudged their tired mothers awake. Those around her started getting up out of their seats and leaving the theater. Impossible. Surely the movie wasn't over already. It was only after she heard the click of the projector turning off that she believed it.

Soon she was the last one sitting among the empty rows. Staying meant she would never make the wrong choice, because she wouldn't make any at all. The characters would be her friends, and the storylines would keep her safe. She smiled. What a headline that would be: "Loony Actress Tries to Live inside Her Films." The studios would love that.

Once, after they had finished school, Owen asked her to think of a story idea on the spot. She wanted to impress him and sound like all the serious authors he devoured, so she started by telling a story about a wealthy family living in a city. But she couldn't think of a decent plot. Owen told her to start again. She launched into a pitch about a woman who lived inside the theater, surviving off the sustenance of stories and sleeping in the stadium seating until the next movie showing. It was a ridiculous scenario and her own wish. Owen had said he liked that one better.

She leaned back against the seat and closed her eyes. Every important memory was somehow tied to him. Time had a way of making all the bad memories fuzzy and leaving only the good in vivid color. She shut her eyes tighter. Goodness, she still loved him. She always had. Every day she thought the pain would lessen. It did, of course it did, but the love remained. It clung to her with as much force as six years ago.

Even if she apologized to him, she didn't know what good it would do. Everyone in the business always said it was who you knew, not what you knew. Her path required connections, didn't it? She frowned at the thought. Then again, any role she won was because of her own work, not someone holding her hand. She might have enough sway in the industry to command the roles she wanted even without outside help.

She stretched her arms and stood up. It wouldn't be long before new viewers would enter the theater. It was time for her fantasy to end, and reality required a paycheck.

Chapter Eight

Owen needed to return a book to Gertrude. Or so he told himself as he left the flat with her novel in hand. Gertrude had loaned the book to him years ago. Every couple of months or so she would remember that he still had it and would ask him to return it. And every time he agreed he would and soon forget. He made long strides over the cobblestone street. It was as good an excuse as any to get out of his flat.

He took the stairs to Gertrude's apartment two at a time. She might not be there. It didn't matter. He was grateful for any reason to get some air. Anything to distract him from the waiting.

Alice, Gertrude's lover, cook, and editor, answered the door. She was a mousy woman, often stooped. Her shoulders were always a little hunched, but a ready smile lit up her features more often than not.

"Hello. Is Gertrude home?" He tried to peer over her shoulder.

"Hello there. She is, in fact."

She pulled open the door wider. He took it as an invitation and walked inside.

"Owen's here," she called into the room.

The flames from the fireplace crackled and hissed. Beside it, Gertrude sat in a giant armchair. Her figure filled the furniture, like the seat had been custom-designed for her. She had the habit of owning a room wherever she went.

She placed her novel face down in her lap. "What is it? I've reached the good part of this story. This better be life or death, Matthews."

He lifted the book he held in his hand. "Wanted to return this to you."

"Oh, is that the Sherwood I let you borrow? Set it on the mantel." She waited for him to put the book down. "Now, why are you really here?"

He straightened his shoulders. "I wanted to return it."

"Don't lie to me. If you wanted to do that, you would have done it a year ago."

A year? Guess she really hadn't cared about it.

"I wanted to get some air."

Alice wheeled in a tray with three cups of tea, and Gertrude's eyes lit up.

"Thank you."

Alice nodded and walked over to the other armchair that sat across from Gertrude's. Without looking up, she resumed her knitting.

"Is this about the actress?" Gertrude said *actress* as if even the sound of it pained her. She had little patience for the profession. To her, movies were a mindless source of entertainment. "I was surprised to see her the other day."

"I don't think you'll be seeing her again."

"And will you be seeing her?"

He stared at the fire. He couldn't outrun Iris at the wrap party. It was far too late to cancel his acceptance. Besides, he believed in honoring his word. If he'd told Pierre he would attend, then he would.

"I liked how she looked at you."

"You must have imagined it. She's chosen someone else."

"Is that what she said?"

"Not in so many words."

"It's never wise to place words in someone else's mouth, I've found. We have a habit of choosing the wrong ones." She dangled her hands over her armrests and clucked her tongue. "No matter. Say, Ezra told me about your rejection."

More salt to rub in his wounds. "Which one?"

"Good art always finds a home. It's not your writing to blame. I gave him your sketch because I liked it. It's a good story. A little too simple for my tastes, but fine for others."

He appreciated her support. His father's friend had introduced him to her when he'd known barely anyone in the city. Attending the parties and discussions at her apartment alone had expanded his literary circle. When his father's friend decided to move back to the States, she had stepped in as his mentor.

"Any improvement in my writing is thanks to your revisions."

"Nonsense. The words came from you, didn't they? Anyhow, Ezra wasn't the only one I showed it to. I sent it off to Max."

"Max who?"

"Perkins. Maxwell Perkins. He's an editor for Scribner's."

The name rang a bell. The man published Scott, if he wasn't mistaken. Scribner's was a reputable publisher, one of the best in America. He steeled himself for another rejection. Forget the best, his manuscripts couldn't even find a home at the mediocre.

"He's interested in meeting you," she continued.

"You can't be serious."

"I wouldn't be so cruel as to joke about that. Yes, Max is interested in meeting you at his office."

"Where?"

"New York."

The city was a world away. Tickets for a passage back home hardly littered the streets. He would have to buy one in advance and make plans for accommodations in the city. It wasn't cheap. He did have his earnings from the screenplay. Then again, using his check wouldn't leave much in the way of savings. He could be buying a ticket to hear another rejection, for all he knew.

She picked up her teacup and took a sip. She made a satisfied sound, closing her eyes. "Excellent tea, Alice." When she opened them, she looked surprised to see Owen still standing there. "You act as if I've given you another rejection."

"No, that's not it. Thank you for showing him my work." The wheels in his mind turned. "But I'm not in New York."

"Then be there. Right now, writing novels is a hobby for you." He cringed.

"Meaning: you can't support yourself through the earnings from your books."

Given that they were nonexistent, he supposed so. Still, it sounded callous to hear it from Gertrude's mouth.

"Your hobby will never turn into a career unless you invest in it. Let me know when you want to contact him."

"You think I should go to New York?"

She picked up her novel and began reading.

"Do you think I should or not?"

She didn't look up from her page. All he wanted was actionable advice, and all she offered were pithy statements like a modern Merlin.

Alice set her knitting aside and offered him the tea.

"Thank you. That's kind of you, but I think I'll show myself out." He had enough to think about for one visit. She called out a good-bye as he left their flat.

New York. It could be another adventure, he mulled to himself as he changed a few hours later for Pierre's party. It was his best shot at a major publication. If Perkins wanted to meet with him, it was an opportunity waiting. There was always the possibility of a familiar outcome: he would show Perkins his manuscripts and Perkins would reject them. But his work would stay rejected regardless of whether he talked to the editor. Perhaps it was worth it to take the risk.

The lapels of his jacket lay smooth against his wool suit. He didn't have time to consider more rejections; he had to attend the wrap party. He slicked his hair back with pomade so that it parted on the side. After a few minutes of digging through his wardrobe, he found a vest. The material was a stark black, contrasting against the grey wool. Still, it was as good as it was going to get for the evening.

The party was at a club off a side street of the Champs-Élysées. During most days, swarms of people surrounded the place. None of them could be seen tonight; it looked like Pierre had rented out the whole venue. A guard stood at the front of the club, making sure everyone was on a specific list for the movie. A red carpet extended down a flight of stairs that led into the main foyer. The dim lighting and smoky air reminded Owen of a jazz club half a block down from his flat. Other than that, the club's interior belonged to a different time. The intricate detailing along the stairwell recalled the Rococo period, and stone pilasters standing at equal intervals against the walls appeared Greco-Roman.

He tried to keep his mind occupied with New York instead of Iris. Easier as an intention than a practice. A small part of him had accepted Pierre's invitation to see her. She had asked if he would be attending, after all. He could even pitch another screenplay to Pierre. A new story idea had been swimming around his head over the past few days. It was a story about a second chance.

He scanned the crowd as he walked into the club, searching for a glimpse of her black hair. A woman dressed in a suit with a top hat held a long cigarette holder, men donned every shade of bowtie in existence, and rows of tables stood covered in both full and empty champagne bottles.

No sight of her or Pierre.

An unmistakable laugh broke out from across the room. He turned his head in its direction. And then he saw Pierre. Iris held a glass of champagne as he filled it. An easy smile lit up her features. She wore a floor-length dress, half covered in sequins and the other half covered in black velvet. Her hair was wrapped in a bun, and her lips were a cherry red. She looked stunning.

He could walk up to Pierre and pitch his story idea. He knew the basic plot in his head. The characters were all laid out for him to bring to life. Yet he stayed frozen, watching them. The tendrils of the plot wilted in his mind. Pierre had something else to occupy him.

He glanced away as soon as she made eye contact with him. Other guests, either supporting actresses or crew members, came up to talk to him. He chatted with the ones he had met before and pretended to know the ones he didn't. Out of the corner of his eye, he could still see Iris and Pierre together. It made him sick. He wanted to apologize for everything, apologize for all of it. She didn't deserve the words he'd thrown at her. But he couldn't say it in front of Pierre.

The din of the night grew rowdier. The champagne started to hit the guests, and some attempted to dance on stage alongside the band. Others dispersed from the party as they took their favorite cast or crew member away for the night. The world under the influence seemed brighter somehow, like every joke was funnier and every gaze more sensuous. Maybe that was how life was supposed to be enjoyed. But did they see the world from a filtered perspective, or did he see it from a muted one?

The woman next to him nudged his arm. Her name was either Adrienne or Agathe; he couldn't remember which. She smelled like she had bathed in perfume right before the party.

When he acknowledged her, she inclined her head in Pierre and Iris's direction. "Have you heard the rumors?"

He feigned ignorance. "I haven't."

Another woman, older than the first, leaned forward. "I heard they were engaged. He's quite a catch. No wonder she lets him hang on to her arm."

"He's a lucky man."

The woman's husband shook his head. "She doesn't want to be engaged, someone told me. I've heard she's simply staying with him in the States. A risqué arrangement, if you ask me, but then again, it was her idea."

Owen wanted to shut out all their nonsense. He didn't know the difference between gossip and fact anymore. That was the worst part of her silence. Against his better judgment, his gaze drifted back to Iris. Pierre remained attached to her side, his hand resting on the inside of her elbow. Her attention looked wrapped up in whatever he told her. When Pierre slid his hand toward hers, Owen looked away. Enough torture for the night.

He excused himself from the group. Coming to the party had been a mistake. Her choice was clear. He had ascended a few steps of the staircase before someone called out his name. He pretended not to hear and continued up the steps. But a dash of footsteps followed his pace.

A hand settled on his shoulder. He looked behind him to see Iris standing on the step beneath his.

"Are you leaving?" she asked.

"Look, I'm very tired and I'm going home."

"You just got here. Do you have to leave now?"

"I can't stand here and watch."

"The party? I can introduce you to anyone you want."

"No, watch you flirting with him. Watch you ... Forget it." He started to turn around. Nothing he said would change anything.

"Pierre? Wait, Owen, just wait a second."

He kept his back to her. His legs itched toward the exit, but he waited for her to continue.

"I really didn't mean what I said the other day."

When he looked over his shoulder, her face looked stricken. He felt an urge to take her into his arms. "I think we both said things we didn't mean."

"You're not angry with me?"

"If he's what you need, I understand."

"But he's not. And if you think I've chosen him over you, you're wrong."

His chest lifted.

"Because the truth is that I will always …"

A gloved hand rested on the inside of her elbow. Her mouth clamped shut. The owner of the glove, Pierre, stood beside her. He looked back and forth between Owen and Iris with a quizzical expression. Owen couldn't even bring himself to hate the man. There was nothing to fault him for other than loving Iris.

"Leaving so soon?" Pierre clapped his free hand on Owen's back. "The party's just begun."

He locked eyes with her. "Would you like me to stay?"

Her lips opened, as if about to say something. He waited. He wanted her to speak. If she asked him to stay, he would. But her gaze averted to her elbow and her lips closed again. Pierre's grip remained firm.

So this was how it would end. No reason to prolong anything. He nodded to both, wished them good night, and ascended the stairwell.

Chapter Nine

Iris commanded her legs to follow him. His frame began to disappear behind the shadows of the stairwell.

"Is there something you would like to tell me?" Pierre asked.

The room started to spin. Owen was gone.

"Be honest with me."

Better to deny it. "It's nothing."

"Do you have feelings for Owen?"

She pressed her lips together.

His voice became low. "Do you or do you not care for him?"

Her attention flickered back to the party. The guests flittered about, throwing back their heads and laughing at someone's joke or leaning onto each other in a drunken stupor. All actors, crew members, producers. The kind of people that, a few years ago, she would have wanted nothing more than to spend the night mingling with. Now it all had a dull sheen.

She had started her career with so much faith in her own capabilities as an actress. When had she started depending on others to make her career for her? It wasn't up to Pierre to make her career; it was up to her. She could achieve success without him propping her up. He could offer her all the leading roles the studios could dole out, connect her with every major director in town, and set her up at the nicest apartment in the hills. He could do all of that, and she would still feel nothing.

"I do. I do have feelings for Owen."

What was holding her back? She didn't need Pierre to hand her what she wanted.

"And I'm going to go to him."

Pierre sighed. "Then go."

Her eyes widened. She couldn't tell if he was joking. She had expected anger. Instead, he looked calm. His shoulders drooped, but no trace of fury lined his voice.

"Go, Iris. I have no desire to keep you here any longer."

Her legs burned to follow his advice. She shifted a look back and forth between the door and Pierre.

He managed a half-smile. "I've enjoyed having you as my lead actress."

"And I can't thank you enough for this opportunity."

"There will be others in your future. Now please, go."

She kissed his cheek. "Thank you."

Her speed picked up as she exited the club and emerged onto the street. Rain pattered onto her skin in tiny flecks. She would be drenched if she didn't find Owen soon. She ran toward the main street and along the Champs-Élysées. Those walking around her began to unfold black umbrellas like a field of dark flowers blooming. It both shielded their clothes from the rain and made it harder for her to see who they were. Could one of them be Owen?

The grey buildings began to give way to a garden. A gazebo at the end of it provided shelter to a group of huddled pedestrians. She squinted at the crowd. No sign of him. She continued along the sidewalk and into the park. A concrete arch and several steps separated the lower park from the upper part, and she descended these steps to cross into the main square. Tall hedges cut into a labyrinth shape greeted her. Despite the empty garden, she kept up her quick pace on the paved path. A growing sense of dread pooled in her stomach. He could have sought shelter in any one of the buildings along the road. She might never find him.

Her dress yanked her back. Its fabric caught in the panels of a grate along the sidewalk, and the ground beneath her feet gave way. She stuck out her arms to try to block her fall. Instead, she landed with a hard thump and a rip of her skirt. Her shins pulsed with a dull pain as she examined the damage. She had scratched the sides of her arms, and a thin line of blood ran down her right forearm.

Someone held out a hand to her.

"It's fine, thank you …" She looked up from the hand to the face of the man extending it to her.

Owen.

It was warm and familiar and safe. It was the face of the boy who had stolen her heart as a teenager, older and roughened now, but still identical to the one in her memories. Still the same boy giving her the same feeling. Her heart slammed against her ribcage.

She took his hand and stood. The fabric stuck in the grate ripped away from her dress, tearing out a chunk. No doubt the bottom of her dress now formed a zigzag edge. It didn't matter. He was here.

"We need to find shelter," he said.

He tried to usher her away and toward the upper floor of the garden, but she resisted. She was tired of waiting. If she didn't say what she needed to say now, there might never be another chance. The rain fell with steadier strokes around them, flattening damp strands to his head.

"Were you planning to not speak to me at all tonight?" she asked. "If I hadn't stopped you, would you have left without saying good-bye?"

He shook his head. "This is how it has to be. You said that once, didn't you?"

He still remembered. "I didn't know how much you meant to me back then. All I saw was my own dream."

"You should be at the party."

"No, I should be here. With you."

"Jesus, Iris, we've tried this before."

"No, we haven't. Not properly. I'm done with us running away from each other. All I need is someone to believe in me as much as I believe in myself. I don't want his connections or film roles. None of that makes my life any better. You do."

"I can't offer you nice restaurants or fancy hotels …"

"I don't care about any of that; I can have that on my own."

"What are you trying to say?"

"I'm saying that I'm here now. I'm here for good."

"I'm sure he's still waiting for you."

"He's not. He knows."

"Knows what?"

"That I love you."

"You love me." He spoke slowly. It was a statement, not a question.

"Yes, I do."

She watched his Adam's apple bob up and down as he gulped. His piercing blue eyes searched hers. She met them with a look of what she hoped was courage. Her knees felt weaker the longer he stared at her. Now she'd done it. There was no going back to being simply past acquaintances. They would either be something or nothing at all. She had handed him the power to respond, good Lord. He could leave her hanging, with either a word of rejection or, worse, no words at all.

Why didn't he say anything?

Her cheeks grew hot. She'd made a fool of herself. "There, now I've said it. You don't have to say it back, of course, there's no reason for you to also reciprocate any feelings I—"

"I love you too."

Her heart soared. He loved her. After all this time, he still loved her. She wanted to hear it again. Her hand reached up to cup his cheek. When he laid his hand over hers, she shivered.

"I love you very much, Iris," he repeated.

He leaned toward her and captured her lips with his. Her toes curled. Owen pressed her tightly against him, his hands settling on her hips. The raindrops started to ease up. By the time she pulled away, only a light drizzle sprinkled onto her cheeks. Their breaths fogged together, emitting human smoke into the night air.

• • •

Owen had always been a planner. In school, he had filled out an agenda for all his assignments. He didn't understand why some of his friends roamed around the city without a destination in mind. He hated the risk of getting lost. Everything he began needed to have a concrete end. Yet as he walked with Iris to her hotel, he couldn't bring himself to think of one.

They passed by a park, two bubbling fountains, and a band playing a bastardized Louis Armstrong song. They held hands tightly. Iris swung their arms together as they walked, casting a "V" shadow against the sidewalk that reminded him of a bird in flight. Three teenagers on their bikes sang an old love song to them as they rode past, cackling as they turned the street corner.

"They're children," he said.

"There's nothing wrong with being a child."

In her hotel room, his story sat on the low table. The front page showcased several scattered coffee rings. He'd written the first draft months ago, staying up past midnight to finish it in a fit of inspiration. He wrote it for himself, a tribute to a woman he used to know. He'd given it to Gertrude on a whim. He would have never imagined it would land in the hands of an editor.

"Owen, come look at this."

He joined Iris next to the door. She held a note in her hand.

"It's from Pierre."

He bristled. If this was a confession of love, he wasn't sure he wanted to hear it. "What's he saying?"

"He's decided to stay back in Paris for another week."

"Was he supposed to leave with you?"

"He was. But that's not it. He wants to know if you'll take his ticket to New York instead."

She had to be joking. He took the note from her. There was Pierre's handwriting all right, the neat cursive spelling out his ticket's availability. How could Owen ever repay him? He looked at her, the note, her again.

"Well?"

He could meet Max Perkins. He could write in Los Angeles. He could be with her. He could make up for lost time, all the time they'd let slip between them.

A grin spread across his face. "I would love to."

"Where are you planning to stay?"

"First, I need to meet an editor in New York. It wouldn't be long, just stopping in the city."

"Oh, an editor wants to publish your book? That's wonderful!"

"Not yet. He read one of my stories and would be interested in seeing more."

"That's a promising start."

"We'll see. Your career's the one that's about to take off. I'm sure directors have taken notice of all your recent roles."

"Hopefully. Or I'll continue to go at it on my own. I don't need Pierre. I used to think I did. But even his introductions or offers won't shape my career. Only I can."

This was the Iris he recognized, fueled by a fire in her belly. It would keep plenty of studio executives on their toes.

"Where would you go after New York?"

He took her hand in his. "I've been thinking about LA."

She kept her voice even, though a matching smile graced her features. "Well, if you ever need a place to stay, I have enough space in my apartment."

"I might take you up on that."

"I'm sorry we'd be leaving Paris, though. You really wanted to move here."

"The city was never my dream. Writing was."

"But you said you wanted to be here for your work."

He laughed. "And I was wrong. I came here in pursuit of becoming a novelist, but I didn't need a place to inspire my best writing. What I needed was a certain person."

She wrapped her arms around him, and he kissed her forehead. It was becoming a reflex. When he held her tighter, she placed her head on his shoulder and made a content sound.

There were some things in life that always felt right to Owen. Writing. Planning. Drinking black coffee once in the morning and once in the evening. Reading the newest novel from a favorite author by firelight. Sketching along the Seine. He had a long list. And yet despite all that was on it, tonight he knew there was one more thing on that list, one thing more important than any of the rest of them: Iris Wong.

About the Author

Pema Donyo is a full-time finance professional, part-time author, and at-all-times coffee lover. She currently lives in San Francisco. Learn more on her website: http://pemadonyo.wordpress.com

Printed in the United States
By Bookmasters